THE BACKSTREETS

THE
BACKSTREETS

A NOVEL FROM XINJIANG

PERHAT TURSUN

TRANSLATED BY

DARREN BYLER AND ANONYMOUS

Columbia University Press *New York*

Columbia University Press wishes to express its appreciation for
assistance given by the Pushkin Fund in the publication of this book.

Columbia University Press
Publishers Since 1893
New York   Chichester, West Sussex
cup.columbia.edu

Library of Congress Cataloging-in-Publication Data
Names: Tursun, Perhat, 1969– author. | Byler, Darren, translator.
Title: The backstreets : a novel from Xinjiang / Perhat Tursun ;
translated by Darren Byler and Anonymous.
Other titles: Chong sheher. English
Description: New York : Columbia University Press, [2022]
Identifiers: LCCN 2021059846 (print) | LCCN 2021059847 (ebook) |
ISBN 9780231202909 (hardback) | ISBN 9780231202916
(trade paperback) | ISBN 9780231554770 (ebook)
Subjects: LCGFT: Novels.
Classification: LCC PL54.69.T87 C4813 2022 (print) |
LCC PL54.69.T87 (ebook) | DDC 894/.3233—dc23/eng/20220301
LC record available at https://lccn.loc.gov/2021059846
LC ebook record available at https://lccn.loc.gov/2021059847

Cover design: Chang Jae Lee
Cover image: Carolyn Drake/Magnum Photos

CONTENTS

Introduction   vii

The Backstreets   1

INTRODUCTION

Since 2017, hundreds of thousands of Uyghurs have been "disappeared" into a widespread system of internment camps in Northwest China—a space known in Chinese by the name Xinjiang or "new frontier." Nearly all Uyghurs, a population of around 12 million people, have an immediate family member who either is interned in a camp or has been forced to work in one. This project affects every aspect of their lives. The phrase "everyone is gone" or "disappeared" (Uy.: *adem yoq*) is something that I heard Uyghurs repeat on a regular basis during my last research trip to Xinjiang in 2018. Across the entire Alaska-sized region, significant segments of the adult population—particularly men between the ages of eighteen and fifty-five—were deemed "extremists" and taken away, leaving behind children who were often sent to residential boarding schools where their native language, Uyghur, is banned.

The "Xinjiang problem," as Uyghur protest is known in Chinese mainstream society, really began in the 1990s, when large numbers of Han people, the majority group in China, arrived in the Uyghur ancestral homeland in Southern Xinjiang for the first time. These settlers came to build infrastructure and begin to extract the oil and natural gas resources in the Uyghur deserts to fuel China's burgeoning export-driven economy. Over the next three decades, the settler populations took over local institutions—the banks, the schools, civil administration—and Uyghurs were pushed out of more autonomous livelihoods into the cities in search of work. What they found in the cities, though, was widespread discrimination. Unlike Han migrants who came to Xinjiang from across the country for lucrative jobs in construction and natural resource industries, Uyghurs found that companies often refused to hire them. Those who were hired were frequently relegated to low-level positions. Rental and house-ownership regulations often prevented Uyghurs from becoming permanent residents in the city, while Han migrant resettlement in Xinjiang cities was encouraged and subsidized by the government. Evictions, land seizures, police brutality, and religious oppression all played a role in an increase in the frequency of Uyghur protests, some of which were violent, and which in some limited cases met international definitions of terrorism. As the Chinese state took up the rhetoric of the global War on Terror emanating from North America and Europe, nearly all forms of Uyghur protest were labeled terrorism, and Uyghurs who defended their Islamic and ethnic traditions were described as extremists. *The Backstreets* responds in oblique ways to this atmosphere of social violence.

In 2014, alarmed by increasingly visible forms of piety among Uyghurs, which authorities conflated with a tendency toward violence, the state declared the People's War on Terror and began to "round up" religious leaders. The mass detention of Muslims was accelerated in 2017, when local leaders received commands from central Chinese state leadership to conduct a mass evaluation of the Uyghur population to determine who was "untrustworthy" (Ch.: *bu fangxin*) because of their affinities to Uyghur traditions and Islamic faith. The police sent the men and women labeled "untrustworthy" either to prison or to the "reeducation" detention system.

The author of this novel, Perhat Tursun, who at the time of his disappearance was not yet fifty years old, was one of those who was first detained and then given a long prison sentence. Tursun is avowedly secular and is not an advocate of ethno-nationalism. He also opposes those who use Islam to justify violence toward non-Muslims. It is unclear why he was targeted, and the details of his detention and sentencing have not been released. It could have been because of an early edition of this novel itself, which he had published in a Uyghur-language online forum at the end of 2013. It could have been because of his other writings, or that he used a virtual private network, or VPN, to read unfiltered news and contact people living outside China. What is clear is that the "reeducation camp" campaign explicitly targeted Uyghurs in positions of social and cultural influence. And Perhat Tursun was certainly one of those people.

The Disappearance of Perhat Tursun

Perhat Tursun is a slight man with a receding hairline. To look at him, you wouldn't know that he is one of the most influential contemporary Uyghur authors in Ürümchi. When I met him for the first time at a reception for a Uyghur-language publishing house in February 2015, his importance was clear from the way other Uyghurs looked at him as he moved through the crowd. He cut a wide swath. After we chatted for a bit, he said he was really bored. He hated formal gatherings and performing for strangers. He left immediately after the ceremony was finished, glad-handing and mumbling under his breath as he shuffled through the banquet hall. Many people stopped to shake his hand as we walked together to his house.

He lived on the twenty-sixth floor of a new apartment building owned by the Uyghur grocery franchise Arman. Many

Uyghur celebrities lived in the building. While we were waiting for the elevator, we nodded at Qeyum Muhemmet, the TV actor who was later sent to a reeducation camp, along with Tursun and more than 400 other public figures, in 2017. Tursun's house smelled more of cigarette smoke than most Uyghur homes. He had some abstract paintings in yellow by a celebrated Uyghur artist, which seemed to reflect the complexity of Uyghur traditional urban architecture. Otherwise, his living room was filled with carpets and a coffee table covered with dried fruit.

In 2014, when I went to Ürümchi to conduct ethnographic fieldwork on the experiences of Uyghur rural-to-urban migrants, one of Tursun's friends, someone I'll refer to as D. M., suggested that I read Tursun's novel *The Backstreets* as a way of understanding how the Uyghur migrant experience had been staged for a more general audience. Over the course of that year, as I read the novel, I began to discuss it with a young Uyghur man who was in a position very similar to the protagonist: an underemployed, alienated young migrant who had recently left his job due to systemic discrimination. Eventually, this fellow reader, A. A., became the co-translator of the novel. We began to meet often to read and talk through some of the more challenging passages of the text.

As the translation progressed, it became clear through both my reading and the responses it elicited in A. A. that this representation of Uyghur male migrant lives resonated across a broad spectrum of experiences. By shifting the frame of the narrative of colonial violence away from the authority of the state toward the work it takes for the colonized to live, *The Backstreets* gave A. A. a new way of speaking and being heard. He said, "I feel as though this book was written just for me." It resonated so strongly with him because the feelings in the narrative were his own feelings; the voice of the protagonist felt like his own voice. Nearly all Uyghur migrants I interviewed said that the experiences of alienation and rejection that I described from the novel resonated with aspects of their own lives: the cruel smiles, the open hostility, the bureaucratic indifference. Reading *The Backstreets* became a method of helping young men to tell their own stories and explore their own life paths. As I wrote in a book titled *Terror Capitalism* that emerged from this research, it enabled them to narrate their own stories as part of a larger shared experience of social violence. The story of *The Backstreets* made sense to them and helped them make sense of their own lives. It also taught A. A. and me the value of friendship and storytelling in coping with isolation—a life practice that became the center of my ethnographic practice and one of the chapters of the book.

D. M. had told Tursun that A. A. and I were working on a translation of the novel. This was why he invited me to visit him after the publishing house reception. He told me he was ecstatic that we were interested in the project and in introducing what he saw as one of his most significant works to the English-speaking world. Over tea and cigarettes, we talked about the way the fog of the city acted as an ambient character. How, in the novel, dehumanization—a process that comes from the way Han Chinese people, the majority group in China, see the Turkic Muslim protagonist as valueless because of his appearance and the language he speaks—was folded into this cold sensation. He said the story drew from his own experiences in Beijing as a college student and in Ürümchi as an office worker. In Beijing, where he was part of the first generation of Uyghur students educated in Chinese outside of the Xinjiang Uyghur Autonomous Region, five of his Uyghur classmates had mental breakdowns due to experiences of dislocation and racialization in a university that was dominated by the norms and values of the majority.

Tursun said he himself had not been mentally stable at times. The experience of seeing this happen to his classmates had an impact on him. It made him want to explain the way alienation is related to mental illness and ethno-nationalism. "I was really influenced by *The Plague*," he said, referencing Albert Camus's existentialist novel about the way ethno-nationalism swept across Europe in the 1940s. "I read and reread it. When I come back to it, I always feel as though every line says something important." He gestured a lot as he talked. When he laughed, his smile looked like it was going to break his face in half. He seemed very honest, with everything appearing on the surface. He listened intently when I spoke, a blank stare mixed with a burning alertness. He seemed like a man starving for life.

Tursun was born in 1969, in a village near the twin cities of Atush and Kashgar, just across the mountains from Kyrgyzstan. Like the majority of his fellow Uyghurs, he grew up at the southern slope of the mountains, among farmers whose lives were shaped by the rhythms of sheep herds and the demands of cotton fields. Images in his prose of the way villagers marked space by the length of songs and the time of day by the slope of the sun and the muezzin's call from the mosque reflect this experience.

Tursun grew up in a Uyghur world, but he was also the son of a schoolteacher who was imprisoned as a suspected counterrevolutionary during the Cultural Revolution. Chinese political history directly shaped his personal biography and his family life, pushing him to think beyond the village and reimagine his place in the world. When Mao Zedong died, China opened up to a new era of market and ideological reforms that allowed Uyghur-language publishing to flourish. By the early 1980s, Uyghur translations of Chinese literary and philosophical texts began to reach even Tursun's small village. It was through these books that Tursun, an aspiring teenage poet, was first exposed to world literature. But it wasn't until he was selected to be in one of the first cohorts of Uyghurs trained in Beijing at Minzu University that he immersed himself in language and thinking outside of Uyghur traditions.

Tahir Hamut, one of Tursun's closest friends, who was also in those first cohorts, remembers those years of discovery very well. Hamut, a prominent poet, filmmaker, and literary critic who found a way to come to the United States in 2017, told me:

> I met Perhat for the first time in February 1988. The first time I met him, I found him to be very melancholy, pessimistic, and restless. But still, he was very warm toward me and other students, who were three years behind him. He suggested that we read more Western literature. This was the first time I heard about modernist literature, Freud, Nietzsche, Dostoevsky, and so on. That is how it began.

This training led Tursun to a PhD in Turkic literature and a dissertation that grappled with the Sufi poetics that formed the basis of Uyghur literary traditions. It also pushed him to become a celebrated poet, novelist, and essayist, often pushing the boundaries of modernist form and, like his Sufi predecessors, the limits of Uyghur propriety.

Tursun never stopped thinking. He had a burning curiosity and aptitude for experimental thinking. Thinking itself, he felt, was the highest human calling. Tursun's office was filled with hundreds of books that helped him do this. He had the works of all of the contemporary Han poets, translations of even the most obscure Nabokov novels and Kafka notebooks. Some of his books were in English, which he read slowly, with great determination and focus. When he lived in Beijing in the 1990s, he became obsessed with going to international bookstores and buying everything he could find. He said:

> I learned a lot from Western philosophy and literature. Particularly Faulkner and Schopenhauer. In high school, I had read a Uyghur translation of Marxist philosophy of dialectical materialism. In that book, they talked about how Plato, Hegel, and Schopenhauer were terrible ideologues. This idea really intrigued me. I thought that because of the way the Marxist book presented them, that there would not be any metaphysical writing available in China. But when I got to Beijing in the mid-'80s, someone told me that these kinds of philosophical works were available in Chinese. I immediately started studying Chinese so that I could read Schopenhauer. I read *The World as Will and Representation* in Chinese. It made me feel as though Chinese was the language of Schopenhauer.

He paused to dwell on this image of the Chinese translation of Schopenhauer's treatise on the essence of objects in the world, his laughter making his words come out like a stutter.

> That is really . . . funny . . . to think about now. After that I read Faulkner, then Camus and Kafka. Eventually I read Freud and Jung and all the other psychoanalytic thinkers too. What I am trying to write about is human experience. I am interested in every form of human thought. I read the scriptures of every faith. I think religion is beautiful. It's like poetry. I believe there is no final truth. And I believe that mental illness has always existed. Mostly it exists in forms of normality. Actually, people that don't fit in with the norms are people who are the least mentally ill. People who see themselves as normal are actually much crazier. I like to write about strange individuals at a particular place and

time in order to show how abnormal mainstream society really is.
I use psychology and literature in my own way in order to diag-
nose the diseases of normality.

Tursun's focus on mental illness, suicide, and alienation—and
his determination to write about obscenity and sexuality in
Uyghur—often made him the target of criticism from more
mainstream Uyghur writers. It made it difficult to publish, but as
work consciously striving to probe the limit of Uyghur thought,
it also made it useful to think with.

In March 2015, Tursun invited me to his house again to discuss
progress on the translation and edits he wanted to make to the
text. His wife made us hand-pulled noodles. We ate and talked
for eight hours. Along the way, we drank two bottles of whiskey.
The drunker he got, the longer his stories became. During one
of his rants, early in the evening before things began to blur and
I forgot to keep notes, he told me, "Milan Kundera, the Czech
writer, is also writing about human experience, but because of his
circumstances, his fiction gets read as somehow political. Actually, it doesn't start with politics, it just gets pulled into it. Human
relationships are the center; they just get blocked by politics. The
same is true for most writers if they're really honest."

But some writers get pulled into political readings more than
others. Because the Uyghurs have been the focus of "counter-
terrorism" campaigns since that way of framing Muslim political life arrived in China following September 11, 2001, nearly all
Uyghur cultural production is viewed as "sensitive." Unlike novels written by Han authors such as Xu Zecheng, who depicts
Han migrant life in *Running Through Beijing*, any depiction of
Uyghur interactions with Han society must account for the way
poverty *and* ethno-racialization produce a cascading effect of

alienation. For Uyghur contemporary authors, urban life is not simply a question of rural-origin class difference, it is a question of epistemic difference and the way their bodies themselves are read. Because Uyghurs speak a different language, cannot pass as Han, and claim a nativeness (Uy: *yerlik*) to their ancestral lands in southern Xinjiang, their encounter with urban Han people is more than simply one of class difference. It is a question of colonial possession and domination, and the way discourse—the permitted speech that shapes social norms—has the power to produce a banal normalization of othering. In this context "Uyghur terrorist" or "extremist" replace older words such as "savage" or "barbarian."

Thinking about the way his identity preceded him, Tursun recalled one of the few times he felt as though Han intellectuals recognized him as a carrier of knowledge.

When I was in Beijing, I took a class with the poet Zhang Zao (张枣). I remember the first time I met him. I told him I liked his work and that I write Uyghur poetry. He said, "Oh, you're Uyghur, what is your name?" I told him Pa-er-ha-ti. And he said, "No, what is your Uyghur name?" That was the first time a Chinese teacher had ever done something like that. Most of the time they would just say, "Oh wow, you have such a strange name," or something like that, but this guy was different. That was already really good, but what he said next really got me. He said that he had just been to Tibet, and he had discovered that Buddhism was not a religion but a philosophy. He said that he really admired the Dalai Lama. Ever since that first meeting we were close. Zhang Zao has since passed away (in 2010)."

Along with the passing of Zhang, the 2010s saw a rise of Han ethno-nationalism that centered on the figure of Xi Jinping and resonated with the 1940's plague described by Camus. To Tursun's thinking this precipitated a profound lack of curiosity regarding Uyghur knowledge. In fact, the existence of Uyghur thought and life itself began to be perceived as a threat.

On January 30, 2018, I received confirmation that Tursun had been disappeared. In early 2020, the news filtered out that he was reportedly given a sixteen-year prison sentence. Tursun will be sixty-seven years old when he is released. The world may never see the five unfinished novels he was working on. He was disappeared at the height of his powers. What remains for now are snatches of his work, most of it yet to be published, and scenes from the world he created. *The Backstreets* is the first piece of his fiction to appear in English translation.

Tursun's disappearance is symptomatic of a greater violence. As D. M., the friend who introduced me to Tursun's work, told me in an interview in 2015 (just as the reeducation camp system was being built):

> People like Perhat miss the 1980s, when no one was willing to listen to someone else's truth. Everyone seemed to think for themselves back then, and no one seemed to be bothered by difference. Now difference is seen as a weakness.

Continuing, D. M. said:

> People don't recognize how bleak the situation is here now, because we don't have dramatic statistics of how many people have died or disappeared. The situation is more complex than this. The way it works is by breaking people's spirit and weakening their sense of self. Suddenly the values that they grew up with seem as though they can be replaced by authoritarian Chinese or

Islamic values. People are becoming empty shells of what they were before. In prison people are taught to think like police. The prisoners are partnered up and chained together. They have to take a shit together. If one of them fucks up, the other one will be blamed. It is a kind of living hell. Although the living conditions themselves are not as bad as they used to be, the psychological torture is more and more sophisticated. Now they try to break your will to live and to have desires.

One time, my friends in prison asked if they could watch Uyghur song and dance videos and the guard said yes. So thirty or so prisoners gathered in one cell and watched the videos. After a few hours, they were happy and were ready to return to their cells, but then the warden said, "No, you asked to watch films, so please keep watching." So they watched the videos for twenty-four hours. Then they asked again if they could leave, because now they were becoming very uncomfortable, but the warden said, "No, you asked for this, please keep watching." In the end, they watched the videos for seventy-two hours. The room was full of shit and piss and thirty men; finally, they said they would never ask to watch films again, and he let them go back to their cells.

Now the government is trying to use education as a tool of assimilating people. But just look at the U.S. In the U.S., Native Americans were forced to forget their languages, forced by the economic system to integrate into mainstream society, but still they maintained their own cultural difference. They wouldn't be assimilated. It will be the same for Uyghurs. All minorities are this way, particularly those that can't pass as the majority. If you are a minority, you will always be a minority. That position cannot be forgotten.

Perhat is a very interesting guy. His novel *The Art of Suicide* was actually put on a list of 100 greatest works of Uyghur culture. But when he heard about this, he was furious. He wrote the Cultural

Bureau a letter and demanded that his work be taken off the list. He said he didn't want that sort of recognition. He didn't want his work to be listed beside all the other propaganda bullshit. Also, he said that his greatest work had not yet been written. He wrote that book when he was twenty-four, and it was just an exercise for him to learn how to write. It should not be taken seriously, he said. He said he didn't want to be famous or popular. He wanted to be a shadowy, marginal figure.

Sometime in 2017, D. M. disappeared into the camps too. In 2018, I found a DVD set of his lectures for sale in a private bookstore in Ürümchi. That was the last time I saw D. M.'s face. Around the same time, the co-translator of this novel, A. A., was also taken. Many of the other young men who taught me how to read *The Backstreets* disappeared into the camps as well. No one knows why, exactly, but it likely had something to do with their digital behavior. For some of them, it was because they prayed and fasted during Ramadan. None of them advocated violence, they were far too terrified. They just wanted to live and think.

Like Tursun, they have become numbered detainees who have to ask permission to take a shit. One by one, the intellectuals who made Perhat cackle with uninhibited laughter began to disappear. Then the young men disappeared in the hundreds of thousands.

The news of Tursun's own disappearance leaked out in coded messages. A mutual acquaintance told Hamut that Tursun had been "hospitalized":

When I heard this, that he had been "hospitalized," I had a really ominous feeling. I felt very sad. I tried to give myself some comfort by thinking that this may be temporary, that Perhat might be released after a while, because I couldn't think of any reason why the authorities would detain and punish him. But I was also very worried because I knew the situation was quite serious at that time and anything could happen. I still remember the anxious insomnia I felt that night. The last time I saw him was around July 10, 2017. No one really knows what has happened to him since.

An image from one of Tursun's most moving poems, "Elegy," rhymes with his own disappearance:

When they search the streets and cannot find my vanished figure
Do you know that I am with you.

(TRANSLATION BY JOSHUA FREEMAN)

READING *THE BACKSTREETS*

Like all great works of art, *The Backstreets* strives to create a world that rivals the reality that confronts it. And in doing so, it also supplements the reader's understanding of history in the making. What I am suggesting is that, like the works that Perhat Tursun was thinking with—Camus's *The Stranger*, Ralph Ellison's *Invisible Man*, J. M. Coetzee's *Life and Times of Michael K.*, and others—*The Backstreets* should be read simultaneously as a slice of history and a prismatic literary fable of the ethnic and racialized outsider. Like these three writer intellectuals, Tursun is using fiction to think, to spin out the logics of a world that he himself has experienced and see where it takes him. Although he does use specific images and scenes of encounter, he is not so much providing documentary evidence of Uyghur life under conditions of colonization as much as portraying it at a symbolic level. Here he is following Camus in showing racial antagonism through forms of existentialist questioning, a kind of idea-driven realism that is both at the level of human experience and beyond it. He is trying to capture something about life that is simultaneously invisible and all too visible. This strategy—at times deadly serious, at others laugh-out-loud absurd, moving in and out of foggy illusory coldness in a kind of waking dream—is precisely what puts Tursun in conversation with authors like Ralph Ellison. The flourishes of language, vivid images, and stream-of-consciousness complexity of the protagonist's inner thoughts define Tursun's style as one that rhymes with Ellison's. But for all of this playfulness, at the edges of his florid speech is a solemnity. Like Ellison—who famously broke with the Communist Party over their failure to address racial prejudice—Tursun is suspicious of ideology that masquerades as truth, suspicious of violent resistance, of false altruism, of easy solutions. He is conscious of who is authorized to speak and for whom. Underneath all of this is a Uyghur lifeworld demanding to be recognized as inextinguishable. Like Coetzee, Tursun uses silence to evoke, but not ventriloquize, those who gaze at the life of the outsider. These silences, too, are full of meaning. The blankness of the gazes that confront the protagonist allude to something deeper, more fundamental to the way Uyghurs experienced the Chinese city.

On April 26, 2014, Xi Jinping, the general secretary of the Chinese Communist Party, urged the general public to turn terrorists into "rats scurrying across a street, with everybody shouting, 'Beat them.' " Over the fifteen years that Perhat Tursun wrote *The Backstreets*, he observed the way this framing of Uyghurs as potentially subhuman was called into being. He watched the way local Communist Party committees, across the Xinjiang Uyghur Autonomous Region, began an art campaign depicting religious Uyghurs as rats being chased by mobs through the streets. He experienced the way Uyghurs were terrified, that is, made the target of a global discourse on terrorism. In China, it is only minorities who are ever referred to as terrorists. A genocidal rage toward Uyghurs—which Tursun depicts by repeating the word "chop" more than 200 times—was generated by the terrorism slot associated with "dangerous" Uyghur masculinity and Islamic practice. This rage, and the smiling condescension of the functionaries who led this campaign, pushed Uyghurs deeper into the gray zones of the city.

The world of *The Backstreets* is a colonial city at the frontier of the Chinese nation, and the book explores the way that city creates dislocated life through the simultaneous pull of beauty and sweetness and the repulsion of hatred and fear. Moving between the big city of Ürümchi, where he tries to find a life; the "stage set" of Beijing, where the protagonist goes to school but does not interact with the Han-dominated city; and a village in Southern Xinjiang where he experienced his first love and violence, the novel develops the themes of the dehumanized outsider and native belonging. Both themes respond to the dispossessing effects of life in the midst of a city that is hostile to Uyghurs. The conflict between these two themes comes together in the form of more general questions about the meaning of life itself.

THE DEHUMANIZED OUTSIDER

The Backstreets follows a night in the life of an unnamed Uyghur man who came to Ürümchi from a village in Southern Xinjiang after finding a temporary job in a government office as a kind of "diversity hire." Because Xinjiang is the ostensible "Uyghur autonomous region," government offices are often legally required to offer a small proportion of jobs to Uyghur employees. Yet, although the region bears the name Uyghur, members of the native or *yerlik* Uyghur population are very rarely placed in positions of real authority.

Over the course of the novel, the sinister smile of the protagonist's Han boss and the revulsion of the urbanites he meets signal that the unnamed man is being dehumanized, seen less as a person and more as a category of being. Slowly, through subtle allusions, *The Backstreets* reveals that it is narrating the experience of being slotted into a subhuman category. Tursun writes:

> Suddenly a rat ran out in front of me like a bullet and disappeared in the garbage. I was stunned for a second, but then kept walking. I was afraid that other people might see the way I had been startled by a rat, so I immediately looked over my shoulder. Just like the rat was skittering around in the trash, I was always skittering around the city. Like him, I would look for food, and after my stomach was full, the greatest desire I had was just to sleep.

He takes on an affect of fear as he scuttles through his office and through the street. Throughout the novel, he appreciates the acute sense of smell that seems to be associated with his difference. The term *smell* appears over 100 times in the novel, often in association with his memories of village life—the turnip cellar, sheep manure, the candy-scented liquor, the neighbor girl's breath—but also with the smell of disease and death that he associates with his office and the atmosphere created by his smiling boss. The freedom that comes from claiming his power of smell and the interior life it inspires has limits. It is made clear that the uniqueness of his self is being stripped away. Over and over, he repeats that he has no friends or enemies, no social relations. He is deeply, and profoundly, alone.

At its heart, then, the novel appears to be about those creatures whose existence is always outside, unwanted. It is about the conditions in which racialized ethnic others always-already know their place in the world. This is shown to them through their social encounters and the structures of power that prevent them from succeeding. To paraphrase the scholar Sara Ahmed, ethno-racialized institutions always take the shape of those in power and make the bodies of minoritized people feel "out of place." In order to prove their worth, minorities often try to prove themselves, over and over again, only to find each time that they are still considered unworthy. Their identity precedes them, a seemingly immutable obstacle to their recognition.

This is the type of feeling that Tursun evokes when he says that the gaze of the protagonist's co-worker "whose skin had a tallowy glow" felt "like rat poison" and prevented him from spending a night in the office. It is also present in the boss, with the ever-present, cruel smile, who gives him assignments as tests of respectability: making him write official letters, forcing him to donate his blood for philanthropic causes. In the voice of the narrator, the hatred that is generated by life in this structure sometimes elicits reactions, "occasionally pushing some to carry out murders and acts of violence, their depression mixed with fanaticism." These reactions are what lead to the "terrorism" label, a self-fulfilling prophecy called into existence by the institutions that excluded Uyghurs in the first place.

For the protagonist of the novel, the inhumanity of the Chinese city builds a deep sense of foreboding. He grasps for anything that might provide him a sense of ownership. The narrative centers on his endless struggle against the pull of social death. His primary strategy is to retreat into his mind, seeking what Søren Kierkegaard, one of Tursun's influences, might refer to as a "negative liberation." But this liberation is always incomplete, always partial; a delay tactic and form of palliative protection. The more the narrator uses a mysticism of numbers—a theme that, like smell, appears in the novel more than 100 times—as a game that might transcend his poverty and his lack of belonging in the ethno-racialized city, the more he realizes his inability to speak and affect the world. His is the choked voice of the trapped. His obsession with numbers is perhaps a way of combating the infinity of the world, the inhumanity of the city. It seems to offer him a path forward, but not a way out. Despite his will to live, his environment continually tells him that he does not deserve a place in the world of the city. The blank silences of the people he encounters suggest that he does not deserve a place anywhere. His inability to even rent a room "the size of a grave" or write his own letter of guarantee, in either Chinese or Uyghur, forces him to conclude that his only and greatest power is simply to live. After all, what outraged his smiling boss the most was that he "was alive." Therefore, his ability to live "must be of great value" and his "existence itself was the greatest source of frustration."

The narrator's lodestar becomes a single drawer in an otherwise locked desk and the numbers on a paper inside the drawer. He is holding on to the promise that the language of science and math might offer a way of overcoming the perceived lack associated with ethnic and rural difference. Yet as the story progresses, it appears that even that source of social belonging—the drawer and the numbers it contains—is under threat. The "respectability" of his education is always unrecognized by his smiling office manager, his gleaming colleague who hisses her morality, even a janitor with perfect Mandarin elocution. Together they remind him constantly of his inadequacy and conspire to complete the process of his social death. In desperation, he begs those he meets on the street to help him, but it is as if his appearance always precedes him, and they either recoil in revulsion or simply ignore him.

NATIVE BELONGING

Yet, if the inhumanity of Uyghur life in Ürümchi is the dominant theme of the novel, the beauty and longing the protagonist expresses by reliving memories of his childhood also form a holding-on-to-life. As he translates the Chinese world around him in his mind, he brings Uyghur knowledge into the present. The narrative of the novel—alternating between the damp office, the foggy street, the postcard-like Beijing, where he and the other Uyghurs never even tried to have a social role, and the beauty and terror of the Uyghur village—is a strategy that pulls time and space in different directions but does not build a fully reliable grounding to the world of the novel. As the protagonist himself notes, "If a mirror is broken into several shards the reality of a scene is also fractured into several pieces, and its reality can never be fully reassembled." Nevertheless, through juxtaposition and flights of the mind, the narrative provides imagistic views of Uyghur village life, placing mundane stories, myths of the desert, the smoke and rituals of village shamans, on the same stage as the philosophers he read in a library in Beijing. In doing this, the narrator constructs a vivid Uyghur sensory experience of objects and actions—a broom fragment, an abandoned shoe, the smell of candy, the sound of a folk song, cracks in the sidewalk. And, to return to what Tursun learned about Schopenhauer's thinking of the world as comprised of objects and their representation, these imagistic portraits of the will or essence of Uyghur things, evoke, from the stage of the novel, the care practices, libidinal norms, relationships with space, and fears at the edge of existential control. Collectively these phenomena represent a world of contemporary Uyghur experience.

The fogginess of the world in the city makes the future appear bleak and hazy, but its indeterminacy also offers a canvas to the protagonist as he runs from the shadow of his alcoholic father and a looming portrait of Mao Zedong. He is running from the underemployment and new forms of misogyny that took hold across the Uyghur homeland in the 1990s, as Uyghurs were pushed off their land and into the embrace of the *baijiu*—the candy-scented sorghum liquor—that was brought by Han settlers. The underlying rot of alcoholism, like the lure of violent fanaticism, and the plague of Han ethnonationalism, looms as a threat to the future of Uyghur survival. These forces stand in opposition to the hunger that drives the protagonist to search for ways out of the cage he finds himself in "without keys or unlocked doors."

The threat of violence also stands in opposition to images of love and beauty that emerge through memories of maternal care, the hot breath of first love, and the lazy, crystalline atmospheres of desert oasis life. The pull of these Uyghur traditions shows that the rhythms of the land and community can create fragile yet durable forms of escape and survival. As such, the world of the novel reflects the richness of Uyghur cultural life while under duress. It comes to life as the narrator moves from strikingly intimate observations to broad thoughts about the meaning of the universe and the place of humans within it. These thoughts come from his own experience as lived through a reading of Uyghur poetics and knowledge systems, Greek sophistry, and modernist philosophy. Here the protagonist demonstrates that though he found no real sense of belonging through his college experience in Beijing—through it and his violent coming of age—he did learn how to play the game of life. Together, these experiences pushed him to develop an interiority that he used to survive in the backstreets of cold, virus-filled Ürümchi.

FURTHER READING

Terror Capitalism: Uyghur Dispossession and Masculinity in a Chinese City (Durham, NC: Duke University Press 2022).

In this monograph, anthropologist Darren Byler utilizes a reading of *The Backstreets* as a way of eliciting responses from young Uyghur male migrants to the city about the alienating effects of urban institutions in Ürümchi.

"Uyghur Literature," in *Pop Culture in Asia and Oceania* ed. Jeremy A. Murray and Kathleen M. Nadeau (Santa Barbara, CA: ABC-CLIO, 2016), 88–91.

In this short overview, leading Uyghur poetry translator and historian Joshua Freeman analyzes the historical role of poetry and prose in Uyghur literary history.

"Fear and oppression in Xinjiang: China's war on Uighur culture," *Financial Times Magazine* (September 11, 2019).

In this article, Christian Shepherd analyzes the causes and effects of the detention of Uyghur cultural leaders post-2017.

"Meet China's Salman Rushdie," *Foreign Policy* (October 1, 2015).

In this essay, Bethany Allen-Ebrahimian considers Perhat Tursun's place in Uyghur intellectual history.

THE BACKSTREETS

The moment I walked out of the office and down the steps at the front of the building, I felt a light shiver. The weather was foul. There was still ample time until sunset, but in Ürümchi, the sun never really rises. It feels like it's always sinking into an overbearing darkness. This makes the city fade into the dimness of imagination, saddening the human spirit. I felt an unexplainable, unforgettable feeling while standing at the front of the building. I stood there looking at the city, but as I was overcome by longing and loneliness, the city gradually faded. The buildings in the distance vanished in the fog.* For an instant I could see the reddish glow of the lit windows, but in the next instant they seemed to disappear. They didn't look like lit windows, they looked instead like the spit of a man whose teeth were bleeding. Everything around me seemed to disappear, and a sudden feeling of horror came over me as if I were trapped, suspended in the air.

I wasn't sure if I had used my right or left foot to cross the threshold of the office door. For a moment I considered

---

* Throughout the novel, Perhat Tursun uses the word "fog" to refer to the industrial pollution that turns the city of Ürümchi, the capital of the Uyghur region, into one of the most polluted cities in the world.

walking back into the office and stepping through the door again. I stopped several times thinking about this. But I didn't turn back and instead continued on my way. When I was a kid, every time I unthinkingly left the house by exiting the gate left foot first, my father would yell at me to come back and start out from the gate again leading with my right foot.

At the time I believed that if someone passed through the gate with their right foot first, their efforts would succeed. If they led with their left, misfortune would befall them. When some kids who had hidden on the roofs along the road throwing clumps of mud at people hit me in the head, cutting my forehead open, or when some kids ran out of the cornfields cursing me, I would think for a while about what might have caused this. Inevitably, I would arrive at the conclusion that all of these things had happened because I had exited the gate without using my right foot first.

Whenever I went outside, I couldn't get over the feeling that there was some kind of misfortune waiting for me, so normally I wouldn't pass over a threshold without using my right foot first. Nevertheless, I would still always doubt whether or not I had actually used my right foot first, which made me anxious. It wasn't just the thresholds of doors. I would also lead with my right foot when I would pass over the shadows of trees along the road or the boundaries of fields. Sometimes if I was going too fast and didn't start with my right foot, I would go back and, assuming the proper posture, start walking again, leading with my right foot. So it was quite clear that when I was passing over the threshold of the office I had used my right foot first. Still, without proof, it was difficult to know with certainty, which made it difficult to be at peace. Floating in that cloud of uncertainty reminded me of the fog of the city. Both feelings were due to the difficulty that comes from proving things that are already very clear.

The fog was becoming increasingly dense. I looked intently at the silhouettes of people in the fog. Some, clad in white and standing one or two meters away from me, seemed to flicker like a reflection in dirty, moving water. They seemed to be walking on air. Those dressed in black you couldn't see until they were right in front of your eyes. I stood there for a while watching people's forms as they passed each other. For some mysterious reason I thought one of them might approach me and speak. I stood there for a long time, but no one addressed me. The shapes seemed to float as they passed by and gradually disappeared.

The endless sound of the cars in the fog could be heard. As this sound mixed with the fog, it made the fog seem even denser. The lights of the cars faded away like the last embers in ashes.

The unceasing sound of the cars was precisely the silence of the city.

It was the silence of the city because the sound of the cars never stopped. This kind of silence was more frightening than no sound at all because it was an unbreakable silence.

Every time I stood in the noise I felt as if I faintly heard a woman screaming in a strangled voice. When I was little, leaning against the big white feedbags, daydreaming while grinding flour, I heard that same voice in the intense rumbling of the mill. When I was watering the crops and stood beside the sluice, listening to the sound of the rushing water, I wasn't sure where exactly it came from, but the faint yet persistent sound of that voice overwhelmed my senses and reverberated in my head. In this sound I could feel endless weeping, the struggles of those who couldn't bear the pain of acute illness. I felt this call drawing me closer. Back then, I would hear it whenever I was in a noisy place. If I wasn't in a noisy place for a long time, it came to me only in dreams. But after I came to the city, I always felt it when

I was walking the streets. That sound mixed with the noise of the cars and gave me no peace. I don't remember who I heard this from, but someone told me that this type of voice brings misfortune. He said most people who die in traffic accidents are killed when crossing the street. They are distracted by this sound and the accident happens when they try to see where it is coming from. The sound is not subsumed in the endless noise of the streets nor the imaginary similarity of it to other distinct sounds. It is the sound of death, calling. But it's not likely that I will have an accident, though, since I don't look to see where the sound is coming from. Because in this city, no one ever calls my name, and I don't recognize anyone.

The license plate number on the rear of a car flashed by in the fog. I felt a sense of unease due to my inability to apprehend it. It was as if I were suddenly lacking something inside. There was no alternative to feeling this. It would be too absurd if I were to run after the car in order to read it. Immediately I focused my attention on how the darkness in my spirit and the darkness around me came together. The empty space that remained from the number of that car also vanished in the fog.

I walked around the square near the office building and onto the main road, following it into the fog. People passed by me. It seemed as though nobody would talk to me, but I couldn't ignore the feeling that somebody might suddenly come up to me and say something.

Today it felt like it was getting dark an hour or two earlier than usual. Perhaps the sun had not yet fully set, I thought. I didn't usually notice the hour at which the sun set, so now I couldn't know for sure if it had set or not. But I felt as though the sun had already gone down. In general, there is never any sunlight in my office, because the window faces mostly to the north and a little to the east. It's a little brighter in the summer, but in the winter when the daylight is very short, I have no choice but to turn on a light during the day. As I sat in that very bright light, I never wanted to look outside. I didn't want to feel the bad feelings that come from looking at the fog of the city. There was a man sitting facing me at the desk opposite. His face always looked like it had been polished to a bright-white sheen. He was always smiling. Except for this man, the office gave me a very intimate feeling. Even when this creature creased its forehead and spoke in annoyed tones, it still seemed to smile. Although the creases around his eyes looked like they were there because he laughed all the time, they actually didn't signify anything other than that this smile had become fixed in place.

It was as if he had adopted that expression when he was a Beijing Opera performer. When he was annoyed, he shook his long, thin thumb and forefinger while he spoke. When he did this, he looked just like someone playing a feminine opera role. The lights in the office seemed to shine a spotlight on his face, making it gleam in a detestable way.

My other two colleagues didn't seem to know what they were doing as they listed along. It was a long time before I could differentiate between my two colleagues. In fact, their faces were not similar at all. Later when I realized this, I was surprised that I hadn't seen the differences between them. It seemed as though they had been poisoned and entered a stupor. They usually looked like they were hurrying to do some task, but the colorlessness of their faces did not correspond with any sort of busyness—instead, they looked like the faces of bloated corpses floating in water. If they were aware of what they were doing, they would have expressed the small signs of being alive that come from a conscious mind. Under their tallowy, smooth, simple, and thick-skinned faces there was no sign of the presence of blood. Even an extreme circumstance would not bring any sort of reaction to their faces. During the first days, the paleness of their faces seemed to be related to the color of the light, but later I gradually came to believe that this was their actual appearance. Even though their faces were so pale, I felt closer to them than to the creature that always laughed, because the gleam of his face made my soul explode.

I always checked the dark corridor when I walked out the door of the office to see if there were one or two mao, or one or two yuan, that someone had dropped, or to see if there were any enticingly dirty things waiting there for me. I often spotted things like thrown-out scraps of magazines, empty envelopes, or handkerchiefs, which allured me with the thought of where they had been. The light in the corridor was usually burned out, but even if the light was working, it was always replaced with another very dim light bulb. It seemed dimmer then than when there were no lights at all. A gaping vacuum always seemed to appear at the end of that elongated corridor, sucking up everything in its sight. I don't know why, but I liked this sucking feeling. Maybe it was because every time I lay half-awake, this same feeling came to me as I fell asleep. It felt like a black hole about to suck me in, but then I would just fall asleep.

I opened the door and investigated the corridor. There was a cigarette butt that had been smoked to the end. But then I looked carefully and noticed that it wasn't a cigarette stub but a bit of a straw mat. Because it was clumped together with some dirt it looked kind of like a cigarette. There didn't seem to be any other scraps of paper in front of the office. I opened the door wider and in the depressing, dim light, I looked into the corridor with more care. What I was looking for was a piece of the cheap, poor-quality paper from the notebooks used by elementary school kids. I had found this kind of paper a couple of times. At first I wasn't interested in it, because that paper wasn't any different than the paper that could be found everywhere in the city: near buildings, on the road, between the bars of a fence, blowing in the wind. It wasn't the kind of paper that would describe someone's inner secrets, disclosing their identity, or a paper from inside an iron chest or a firmly locked cabinet. So I just passed over those kinds of papers without a second glance. But as I walked into the office this morning, suddenly I had noticed a pile of such paper, just lying there near the door. When I stepped on it, it seemed to moan, and so I looked down. There were rows of numbers written on it. A grandfather who had noticed me opened the door to let me in. So, using a great deal of effort, I escaped the desire to know what those numbers meant, closed the door, and walked in. I worried about this foolishness for a moment. I wanted to suddenly walk back, pick up the crumpled, dirty papers, and brush away the footprints on them with my paw. I would look at them one by one. But then immediately I threw myself into the office and shut the door. The shuffling sound of the footsteps of the grandfather who opened the door for me every day grew fainter and fainter, but I didn't dare look out the door. As I was brushing the desk, I felt as though it was getting dirtier and dirtier the more I brushed. I noticed the smell of the water from the mop bucket. That smell seeped into my shrunken intestines and deeper into my colon, making my feet feel powerless. Yet, still, all of my desire was concentrated on that paper in front of the door. I came to the conclusion that I wasn't going to pick it up and give it a look. In the end, though, I failed, because the numbers on the paper were continuously flying in front of my eyes, forming different shapes and orders. The power of that paper made my disposition itch— it couldn't stand those numbers. My colleagues started coming in one by one. Every time someone opened or closed the door, my eyes naturally fell on that paper under their feet. I looked carefully at the people around me and walked to the door when they weren't paying attention. I opened the door and, without picking it up, looked at the numbers on it. I lost myself in the numbers. The relationships between the numbers intoxicated me. I looked at the numbers on the paper and stood there dumfounded, because I noticed that three numbers, written in pencil, were 1, 6, and 9. This was my height. This number bent my knees without resistance and compelled me to bend toward the ground. The repetition of the numbers 6 and 9 made me surrender even more. I was told that this was my weight when I had gone to have a health checkup the day before. I went to this checkup because the office had mobilized us to donate blood. I had always sensed that I was directly related to a bunch of numbers. I didn't arrange all of these relationships between myself and numbers consciously. It wouldn't have been possible for me to arrange them like that. For example, I was born in sixty-nine and my height was one meter and sixty-nine centimeters. And from the gate of the office building to the room where I worked it was exactly sixty-nine steps. In my mind the numbers six and nine were related to my fate very firmly. Moreover, this number read as sixty-nine even if it was flipped over. So it gave me a sign of many things. The number that came next, two and one, was exactly my age. I immediately picked up the paper and looked at my colleagues in the office. Nobody had noticed me.

When I walked the streets of Ürümchi, everything seemed to float in the fog. I felt as though my own body was the only thing with weight. It didn't move from one place to another; instead it sunk into place. The sound of the cars penetrated my heavy body, unsettling me and weighing my body down as I walked.

A man with an exaggeratedly wide forehead and tiny chin suddenly appeared from a place in the fog that appeared denser. It seemed as though the fog had been mixed with other vapors that couldn't be clearly discerned.

Chop the people from the Six Cities,* chop, chop. . . .

He repeated this word "chop, chop," without adding a single letter, while going a distance of about one kilometer. If someone looked at the man's face every time the word "chop" passed his lips, he would see that in the man's imagination, he was chopping

---

* The "Six Cities," or Alte Sheher, refers to the six oases—Turpan, Korla, Aksu, Kashgar, Yarkand, and Hotan—that form the ancestral homeland of the Uyghurs.

people. Every time he said the word, the onlooker would see the glimmer of a bloody cleaver or ax that the man was lifting and slamming down. Every time he blurted out that word, he said the closed-lip consonant "p" with so much strength that following the irate closing of his lips, his whole head trembled.* Every time he said the word "chop," in his mind a man's head was being cut off to roll on the ground, covered with blood. I couldn't be sure, even though I looked very carefully at him, who he was really talking to. At first glance it appeared that he was talking to himself, and with the next glance it seemed like he was talking to a woman walking by his side. I couldn't be sure if the woman dressed in black was walking with him. Sometimes she drifted close to him and sometimes farther away, so I didn't know if he was walking with her or alone.

The cities he was talking about had a population of at least four and a half million Uyghurs. Even his grandson's life span would not give him enough time to sort each of these four and a half million persons into friend and enemy categories. So it seemed that rather than wasting his time with that, he had made peace with being the enemy of the whole population of the Six Cities. Still, it would only be possible to erase all of the people from the Six Cities if they would come to him, line up, and wait for his great cleavers to fall on their heads!

If he rushed in his passion and didn't land the cleaver on just the right place on their necks, they might not be killed. So he would need to measure properly and make sure the cleaver didn't get stuck in the neck bones. He would need to calculate the additional minute it would take to get the cleaver unstuck from each person's neck. For four and a half million people it could be as

---

* By noting that the initial consonant of the word "chop" is "p," the author is specifying that the speaker was saying the Mandarin word *pi*.

long as seventy-five thousand hours. Even if he worked hard every day, he would need to use up his entire life in order to kill that many people. In order to preserve his body, he would need to eat three meals a day and take breaks every once in a while when his hands grew exhausted. If he shortened his life span by losing sleep, who would be left to chop the people from the Six Cities? So he would have to sleep at night. Excluding these periods of time, we can assume that the net time spent by the cleaver hitting necks would be eight hours per day. So he would need 9,375 days. If we broke this number down into years, it would be twenty-five years, eight months, and four days. But I could see that this man, who had already fallen into such an open rage, might not live for another twenty-five years, eight months, and four days. It wasn't hard to see from his face that his anger was wearing down his soul. It looked like it was a straw roof being blown by the wind, or like perhaps it was being eaten out by a worm.

Moreover, the average age of the population was declining. When I was a kid, it was common to see men and women who were over one hundred years old everywhere you turned. Now you can't find even one in a whole village. Some view this as a result of crops being grown with chemical fertilizers. I think the decline in the longevity of the population is due to psychological pressure. Especially the paranoid and hysterical dissatisfaction that comes from the desire to kill being suppressed by modern civilization. An animosity toward the city might also be caused by this.

I had never seen him before, the man whose forehead was swelling wider and wider, and whose chin was receding more and more. Now he disappeared into the fog. After a while, perhaps I would forget that I had seen him. Even if I met him a second time, it wasn't clear that I would recognize him. Perhaps over the course of my life I wouldn't have the chance to meet him again. But I was always-already the one he was going to chop, even though we didn't know each other.

I stopped for a while at the intersection of the streets and looked in each direction. The mouth of the street on the right seemed to be part of a face fading into carelessness in the fog. The mouth of the street on the left side couldn't be seen. Only the turning cars implied that there was a street opening its mouth secretly and copiously swallowing things.

I stopped at the intersection for a while to consider which way to walk. I looked one by one at the names of the streets, the traffic signs along the road, the store signs, and even the bill-boards. I was looking for a clear sign to appear in all of the numbers on them. As if deliberately hiding the parts that had things written on them, the darkest and densest parts of the fog covered up the signs. After a while, as I peered into the void, I felt as though they were forming the vague shape of a woman's body behind a thick window curtain as seen from a distance. I needed to walk nearer to them to look. Among these numbers, only one number was the one I was looking for. But in a split second I lost that number. In order not to start walking with my left foot first, I had looked down at the unclear lines cutting through the concrete. I always stepped first with my right foot, not only when it came to bigger streets but also with the cracks on the narrow sidewalks in residential areas. When I lifted my head again, I couldn't find the number. So I just chose a direction at random.

The fog in the back streets of the city seemed denser than in other places. The fog seemed like it couldn't be contained by the narrow, winding streets. Because of this, it looked even darker. A light hanging in front of a door just a short distance away melded into the fog, as if it was not a light but reddish fog floating in gray fog. The part at the center of it resembled the light red color unintentionally revealed on the clothes of a woman who was having her period. Farther from the center, the reddishness became fainter and gradually disappeared in the darkness.

The disorderly heights of the houses along the street also made me think about the city's old sewage system. Even though this was the first time I had walked along this street, I had heard a lot about it, so I had mentally prepared for it. Maybe because I recalled this, the street felt more winding to me. Or perhaps it was always this winding. But I couldn't believe that the greatest forms of beauty and most famous swindles had originated in this decrepit alleyway. The things that ceaselessly drew people to the city were those two things. At this moment, the unending fog burst the dreams of people, shattering the glow of beauty and crime, erasing it from the surface of the earth.

I don't know anyone in this strange city, so it's impossible for me to be friends or enemies with anyone.

The smell of paint was coming from somewhere. I don't know why, but the smell of paint has always seemed very fragrant to me, ever since I was little. Some people feel uncomfortable with this smell. Some people even think it's poisonous. I don't understand why they feel that way. It's a miracle that the same thing can produce such different effects in people. Most people would be very upset with this. They imagine that everyone has the same responses to the same things. People seem to be endlessly searching for miracles in the world, but when they find one it angers them.

This particular smell of the city, which bothers so many people, excited me no less than the smell of perfume or naked pictures.

Now the fog was slowly flowing like filthy water in a ditch along the narrow street. The shapes of people were floating past each other like debris in the water, with a slow but shivering force. The lights of cars were like red tissues floating in the water or decomposing rags moving slowly through space. I felt like I would choke in the sewage of this road.

I missed the wide, white hillsides, the sand that rises up everywhere along clean village roads, the bright yellow of the fields of ripened wheat, the combined rumbling in the stifling heat of the threshing field, the itching feeling that comes from the urine of the donkeys as they circle the threshing machine, and the strange imaginary things that emerged from my over-heated brain. These things always came to my mind's eye when I wanted to comfort myself, or at least for a moment forget the threat of the infinite fog in front me. But I couldn't really visualize any of these things. The only place I could visualize that was full of light was my office on the dim, damp side of my building. Although it never sees the light of day, it is bright white because of the artificial light. I still don't have a key. Every morning when I go to the office I have to wait for others to open the door. I would find pleasure in pacing the dark corridor while I waited for my colleagues to arrive and open it. Sometimes I would hum a song, but if I heard someone's footsteps I would worry that they might notice my happiness, and so I would stop immediately. For me this itself was enough, I didn't want anything more than this. What does it matter if I don't have a key? It would be the same anyway. I would still go into the office after the others had opened it.

I liked everything in this office except for the worrying smile on that imposter's face as he sat facing me in front of my desk. It was as if I had been living among these things for a long time. That smiling-faced person had conferred the work desk to me. Every drawer of the desk was locked. Only one small drawer on the left side was open. It was so old and rickety it couldn't be locked, so for this reason it was ignored. Its width was one hand-span. Its length was two handspans. The paint on its surface was faded. That rickety, fall-on-the-floor drawer was the only thing in this city that belonged to me. In the drawer I put those few books that made up all of my belongings. Even if one of those books went missing after a day or two, I wouldn't be very upset. I didn't even consider locking the unlocked drawer, because I didn't have any sex paraphernalia to hide like other people. The only thing that I could hide from others was my nude body. I hid that under a sweater whose sleeves seemed to have grown shorter due to their missing threads, pants with stretched-out knees that made my legs look crooked, and a long coat that didn't show its filth due to its blackness.

The smiling face in front of my desk had explained to me that our office's economic situation was not good, so they couldn't offer me a room. I would need to arrange my own housing, he said. I was very surprised when I heard him say this. I walked all over the three floors of the building. After I saw that there were so many wide-open, empty spaces, I couldn't believe that they didn't have a place to fit my thin body. But the happy-faced person facing me wouldn't agree with the idea of me putting a bed in any small corner. At that time, I just wanted a small space— the space a person would need in a graveyard. I would have been satisfied with that. At first a space for one bed, and then a space to hang my clothes, and then a desk for eating and other tasks, and then a space for preparing food, and then one separate room, and then a whole house with a bathroom and kitchen . . . the more the space was owned, the more the need for space would arise. Maybe it would become an insatiable, abnormal need in the end. But I didn't have a desire to own more and more space like this. Some people aren't satisfied with one apartment, they want a whole building and then a whole district. Even after they own a whole city, their desire for more wouldn't be satiated. But I'm not like that. I'm quite satisfied with a one handspan width by two handspan length rickety old drawer. Due to my appreciation of this, I didn't demand anything bigger for a month. In this big city, if my desire grew from one drawer to one bed, perhaps it wouldn't be seen as being hungry eyed. The beds in the cheapest private hotels never belonged to me, and it gradually became clear that I would want one for myself. I couldn't live depending on only just one drawer.

Even though it was made up of tangible things like buildings, roads, and sewage drains, the big city hadn't become something I could really see and touch. Except for that drawer, everything else was just some kind proposition or mysterious incantation. At that moment, as I was walking down the street with my brain full of numbers, the thick fog seeped into my body and soul— fighting to make all of those numbers appear vague. The city where my drawer was located started to become a vague pile of fragmentary shadows. I also seemed to be disappearing among those shadows, walking into that threat.

I felt I had come to a truly big city for the first time only after I arrived in Ürümchi. I looked around worriedly when I heard the sounds of people yelling to one another: sometimes from the right, sometimes from the left, sometimes from behind and sometimes in front. Somehow the sound of the cars suddenly seemed to grow stronger—seeping into my veins and, along with my blood, getting stuck in my brain. As if I were a rat, I imagined the way countless wheels would skid, grabbing the asphalt, shaking, watching the wheels of the cars roll by at extreme speeds. If I were hit by any of those cars, the people inside wouldn't have even a second to see me get hammered onto the ground. In a second, only a black skin would remain, under the countless wheels the hair on my skin would vanish. Then my skin itself would be turned to dust and that rat would vanish into the air. Actually, five years before, I had been to a city several times larger than this one. But only after I came here did I feel as though I had truly arrived in a big city. Over my five years in college, that huge and cold city was just a stage set for me. It was as if an unaccomplished painter had poorly painted a car on a huge canvas, and through a window-shaped hole in the canvas, people were squeezing their heads through the car window, so that it appeared as if they were sitting in the car having their picture taken.

For me, Beijing was a stage set that included about a dozen people. We were twelve classmates in a single class, along with several teachers who came into the classroom wearing shorts, leaving their upper bodies naked, making the city even colder. Over the next few years, I didn't become well acquainted with anyone, except for a few people who came from the same place I was from. Furthermore, I felt as though it was deceptive of others to get acquainted and commiserate with one another. In that big city, only those twelve classmates existed as a part of my life. It was as if, except for them, the ten million people in the city didn't exist for me. My life with those twelve students was actually smaller than the small village I was from. There was a chef in the cafeteria who always threw me my bowl angrily after slopping in my meal. There was the secretary who passed out the meal tickets. At the entrances to the lecture halls there was a staff person who checked whether we were wearing our school badges or not. There was a woman in the library who had a face full of pimples of all sizes. All of them appeared and disappeared around us like shadows. I didn't know anything about them. After waiting in long lines to eat, it was even murky to us who made the food. Our communication with the outside world happened solely inside an envelope. When I sent letters I would never go to the post office. I would just throw the letter into a mailbox in the front of the lecture hall. Another shadow was the obese staff person who gave us fines along the walkway. I was never given a fine even though I spat on the ground. If other students would just make a hocking sound, she would come running looking for the spit. The deliberative actions of other students seemed to indicate that they had persuaded themselves that they were living in the same city as that woman.

I looked at my wrist to see what time it was, but there was no watch on my wrist. I was surprised that I was looking at my wrist for a watch that had never existed. Maybe what I wanted to look at was a watch that was drawn with blue ink on my wrist. I didn't remember who drew the watch on my wrist, but so that it wouldn't fade away, I refused to let water touch my wrist for a long time. Eventually though, that blue-ink watch disappeared in its competition with the grime on my wrist. As if I wanted to hide my fingers, I stretched the sleeves of my jacket to their tips and continued down the road.

Like the eyes of a lecherous man who couldn't control his lust, the windows shone vaguely with greed—the capillaries of the eyes already enlarged and turning red.

Something was rustling in the trash in front of the wall along the edge of the road, which was crumbling, leaving gaping holes in the bricks. Suddenly a rat ran out in front of me like a bullet and disappeared in the garbage. I was stunned for a second, but then kept walking. I was afraid that other people might see the way I had been startled by a rat, so I immediately looked around over my shoulders. Just like the rat was skittering around in the trash, I was always skittering around the city. Like him I would look for food, and after my stomach was full, the greatest desire I had was just to sleep. I didn't know of anything better than sleeping. I couldn't even fantasize about any sort of sexual longing. There was nothing greater than feeling the fog, the desire and frustration that comes from the seductive illusion of the big city and floating among the figures on the road. Up to that point I hadn't realized that there was any reason to determine whether sleeping or filling my stomach was the greater need. I don't know why people always feel disgusted if the need to fill one's stomach is mentioned directly. Instead, many different kinds of metaphors, political speech, and scientific terminology are used to venerate this need, making it seem like something sacred. When we were kids and heard myths told by others, I thought that the objects in them, such as carpets, gold, bronze, and pearls, were edible. Later, as I grew up, and I realized that those things weren't edible, I was surprised. Why did people see those things as so valuable even though they weren't edible? For a sickly child who always walked around hungry, unable to get hard corn bread down his throat, something edible was always precious.

I couldn't even manage to do things like sleeping and mating with the opposite sex. Vermin could sleep in any hole, any place they end up, and they could mate with females anywhere. But I couldn't. Maybe that is the cost of being human.

Two people passed by me, their faces made of iron, their eyes staring straight forward as if fixed on an approaching target.

There was something lying in the road a few paces in front of me that I couldn't recognize. I thought it was possibly the prone body of a rat, but after I got a bit closer I realized it was part of an abandoned sorghum-husk broom. The head of the broom was almost worn out. Its owner didn't want to abandon it until it could absolutely not sweep a thing. Even after it was totally useless, its owner still used it for a time. The handle of the broom was worn down to the size of the body of a rat. At first I didn't think it was detached from the other parts of the broom, but after I got closer and looked carefully, I realized it was actually the broom stump. One side of it was black, as if it had been burned. Maybe it had been used for ceremonial burning. If it hadn't been used as part of a Uyghur smoke ritual, why would its one side be burned? Once this came to my mind I immediately stopped and looked in every direction. If I found another burned bit of the broom, I could be certain that someone had actually used it in this way. Despite the incongruity of this line of thinking, which was odd to consider in the city, the broom stump was becoming more and more mysterious in the fog. So I searched around for other parts of the broom. There was nothing to be seen of that broom. It was completely impossible to search it out. The appropriateness of seeking it was like that of a herder taking his livestock through the village while his strong songs spread over the land to distant places in the clear air of dusk, or the hidden whisperings and soft cries under a desert date tree as the moon spread its cold light in the bright night. But the hungry, voracious fog was swallowing my last thoughts about the light.

I think that the estrangement, fear, and discomfort Uyghur boys face when they come to the big city is a result of them mistakenly thinking that the city resembles the beauty of a woman. In their minds, only city women are distinguished by their white-boned, aristocratic lustfulness. It is as if they have nothing else to do besides seducing men. They don't get burned out with work and their bodies don't lose their shape. You can see the blood pulsing through their bodies through their thin, translucent skin. What is most surprising about this is that the dirtier the city actually becomes with its filthy fog, polluted air, its piles of trash, and so on, the more gorgeous the women in this big city become. As if the manure and trash made the flowers grow more vigorously, like the pollution and grime made them more beautiful.

I would always hear people cursing the city with their insults. The reason they hated the city was because their desire for the city went beyond all limits . . . they lost themselves in their dreams, and without knowing it, became resentful.

I tried to imagine female shamans with their foaming mouths, the skin on their faces peeling, their whole bodies shaking uncontrollably, as the top of the broom was burning in the house, purifying it with the fragrant smell of the smoke. But the fog that was filling the city was stuck in my brain and taking over my thoughts. As it became even denser, I couldn't visualize a single aspect of that scene.

The tops of the buildings were disappearing in the fog. Smaller buildings and single-floor houses also seemed to be incomplete, as if just part of them remained while the rest had evaporated. In the fog, only the sound of the cars on the main roads confirmed that this was a metropolis. I couldn't help but feel that this place was an infinite ruin.

I saw an abandoned triangular piece of wood on the road that was perhaps part of a desk, chair, bookshelf, or a woman's armoire. The one side was painted a liver shade, which was very faded. Perhaps it broke into a triangular shape due to carelessness. Since the side on which it was broken was quite clean, while the other sides were very dirty, it was clear that it had happened quite recently. I imagined a desk that might have been made whole with that piece of wood. Perhaps since the desk was like the one I received through so much struggle, the piece of wood had the power to attract a person to this city. This thinking suddenly made me anxious. I felt as if that abandoned piece of wood on the ground was like a piece of the desk in my office. I immediately wanted to go to the office and look at it . . . but it was clear that this corner of a board was not part of my desk.

I looked around in the fog and I tried to guess where my office was located, but I couldn't remember. I had totally lost my sense of direction.

The fog slowly seeped in through my sleeves and the openings of my clothes, stroking my body with its cold substance. Even without this embrace, I was a cold-blooded person. If I stay in the cold I just shrivel up. Although someone else might feel comfortable in cool weather, I always feel uncomfortable. When others see me they ask: "Are you sick? This is a symptom of sickness that can't be ignored," they say. Then my body feels like it was being taken over by a plague. Perhaps at this moment the virus was moving anxiously in my body . . . After the fog seeping into my body met the virus, it forced the virus to be excreted from my body back into the fog, making it even colder and murkier. . . .

I don't know anyone in this strange city, so it's impossible for me to be friends or enemies with anyone.

The fog gradually became denser, making everything disappear. Except for a few murky places, in the back streets everything was surrounded by the fog—vanishing in what seemed to be the infinite border of the world. I felt as though the buildings behind those lit windows, which seemed to float in the fog as murky light-red bloodstains that couldn't be easily washed away, were unimaginable. I struggled to sense that somewhere out there I had an office, and in the office I had a desk, and in the desk I had a drawer.

At this moment I realized that the whole universe was composed of numbers. Maybe I myself was composed of numbers. Maybe my soul had led me to this place because of its desire to become one with the countless numbers of the universe.

I had put the paper with those numbers written on it in the drawer that belonged to me. When I was sitting at my desk I always opened the drawer and, without taking the paper out, I would guess at the meanings of the numbers on that paper that was smudged with footprints and gapped in places where it had gotten ripped by something.

One, seven, three, nine. I thought that this number signified something to do with my fate. Maybe it meant I was going to be a wanderer between the ages of seventeen and nineteen. It was true that I had left home at seventeen years of age. Maybe it didn't mean that. Maybe it meant that my final day would be when I turned seventeen on the ninth of March. But that day had passed and I hadn't died. I was surprised to have thought that day might have been when my days would be completed. In order to get this thought out of my brain I walked over to the dirty window and looked out. Like a strangled sound, the window made the outside even vaguer than the fog floating in the dim city. I noticed the license plate number of a passing car. Eight, seven, five, four. This number wasn't on the paper. What did it mean? I would die on the seventh day of September, at four minutes past five? No, it wasn't that. The most recent seventh day of September had already passed peacefully. It would be a fairly long time until the next seventh day of September would come. By that time this sign would be canceled. As if someone might detect my thoughts, I looked around at my colleagues.

When I sat in the office I always had the fantasy that my body had a relationship with everything else in the office. But they never encountered each other and remained alone as separate things. At that moment, as I was walking in the fog, I felt as though my body was becoming part of the fog or that the fog was becoming part of my body. Usually a man would sense that only viruses could become a single substance with a body, otherwise the world of inert matter and the cold city would repulsively exist outside of the body. Now though, they were acting like viruses that slowly seep into the body and becoming part of it. As this happens a person comes to believe that viruses aren't alien to the body but rather of the body itself. Just as viruses have become part of my body, so the fog was slowly seeping into my body and becoming part of it. My body also was slowly breaking the limits of sense and shape as it slowly evaporated into the fog. At that moment I wasn't clear on whether or not my body was becoming fog or the fog was enveloping my body—this hesitation and the vagueness of the sensation made me feel as though I was a single substance with the fog.

Earlier, when I had dreamed about big cities, I first thought about the threat of being lost. After I grew up, I found out that being lost was just for kids. Actually, there are no mysterious places out there, people just made that up due to their desire to lose themselves. In the big city there are names for every street, every residential area and building, so even when I lost my direction I was still never really lost. Yet, even though I knew this, I always still felt a sense of threat. Perhaps this is because I had grown accustomed to an inescapable threat of being lost over a long period of time when I was a kid.

I recalled the numbers I had seen that morning on the paper in front of the office door and tried to connect them to a number that might be related to my future residence. But the more I walked in the fog and the more vague the scene around me became, the less certain I was of the assumptions I had made earlier. I felt a sense of horror as they began to transform themselves from conclusions to assumptions to doubts.

I recalled what the person said when I was trying to rent an apartment, that my future home would be on this exact street. But walking in the fog the scene became murkier and my assumptions also gradually were weakened from conviction to assumption, and from assumption to suspicion, and this made me hesitate.

When the shape of a man suddenly appeared in the fog and came close to me, I tried to ask him for directions, but when I paused he immediately quickened his steps and passed me. It seemed as though he intuited what I wanted and intentionally avoided me. So after he passed me, I didn't want to call after him. Immediately following this, another tall and listing man appeared. So I didn't need to call that first person to stop, I just asked the second one.

After the tall person listened to my question, he stood blankly with his mouth open for a while. Although the fog and the darkness made everything gloomier, it seemed as though I could clearly see every line, pore, and yellowing hair on his face. The strange look of him confused me. From his appearance it seemed as though he had some sort of mysterious sickness or mental deficiency.

I repeated my words again thinking he didn't understand. But he still stood stone-still as if cursed—like it was unimaginable that someone might ask for directions.

I stood there with an inquisitive look on my face and then immediately looked away because I was uncomfortable. As if he suddenly came to consciousness, he shut his big, gaping mouth and immediately turned and walked away. Even though I didn't look, I felt as though after he had walked a few steps he might have looked back at me anxiously.

I couldn't get over the uncomfortable feeling that creature's appearance had given me. After a while, his face, which had been seared in my brain, became murky and gradually vanished.

The road smelled like rotten food. I didn't know where exactly this smell was coming from. Maybe there was an unseen ditch nearby. Maybe people threw their leftovers there every day. There was no sign of a drain on this back street. Maybe the urban sewage system, which was the most important part of a big city's way of life, was not hooked up on this street. Every time we mention the city, people's first thoughts are of the youthful women of these back streets, their clothes revealing their bodies and flashing their pure white bare legs as they cross the street. It is as if the essence of the city was concentrated here in this place. The image of the city cannot be separated from our imagination of this street. So I couldn't believe that this street still didn't have any sewage pipes.

Because of the thick fog, the reddish lights from the windows along the street were trapped in the narrow area and couldn't dissipate further. The old, dilapidated condition of the walls of houses could be seen from the way the plaster was crumbling under the lights. The windows looked like gloomy gashes on the body of a man who had been beaten to death—giving off a sad feeling. The light floated away like gradually clearing yellowish pus from those gashes.

This street seemed to be at the limit of an earlier time when nothing existed, and the universe was just being created. I felt myself seeking a sign of truth about creation from the murky fog. My little body was very weakly trembling, as if being choked in the amniotic fluid of a womb. Every gash seemed like an open door to me, but I didn't have the courage to walk through.

I hit something with my foot, making it clatter. I glanced down and noticed that it was a tangled up cable that perhaps someone had used for tying together the opening of something.

It wasn't clear if there were words written on the discarded papers that were scattered here and there on the road. I was disgusted by the way their color had been transformed by sand, mud, and filthy water. Because of their disorder and fragmented condition, there was hardly any sign that distinguish them as papers.

One of them was folded multiple times into an elongated shape—its middle part seemed to be glued together while its two edges were clearly distinguished, broad ends. From one glance it could be seen that the middle part had clearly defined dark bloodstains. Since it couldn't be seen very clearly in the dark, it was impossible to know if it was tissue paper or a woman's hygienic pad. It was hard to see the color of the blood on the paper, but it wasn't hard to assume that it was stained with blood.

A new disgusting smell entered my brain from my nose and disturbed my senses. Then I realized that there was a toilet at the side of the road. The walls of the toilet seemed to tilt as though they were leaning. They seemed to be quite old. Even with its strong, disgusting smell, it seemed to have been forgotten by humankind. All around it were discarded things. Although the walls were crumbling to such a large extent, they had never been repaired. The color of the reddish bricks might have been made black because of the disgusting smell. The original color couldn't be seen. The words written on the black walls expressed sexual hunger and frustration. There were also all kinds of drawings and sex symbols. Perhaps because they were written with white chalk, they could be clearly seen in the fog. Or perhaps it wasn't because of the white chalk, but rather because of people's sensitivity and desire for the meaning conveyed by those things. People's eyes don't even notice the missing parts of these words and drawings. They fill them in automatically themselves. The exaggeration that comes from mysterious feelings and gaps in the experience of the children who draw these things, combined with the experience of adults, produce this phenomenon as a whole.

At this moment a woman was walking down the three steps of the restroom. Since the steps were worn from the difficult hobbling of hurrying high heels, the edges were narrowed and rounded, making the length between each step undistinguishable. They could only be differentiated by the height of their slope. There was a brick that was broken in half on the left side of the second step. On the right side there was also a fairly large section of the bricks that had fallen down. I don't know why, but I thought that these steps might have been built that way. I might have thought this because of the character trait I received from my father of not admitting to the passage of time. I have never wanted to admit that things have some kind of past. It's as if when I see a thing it is always already in its original condition and never had a different state of being.

The woman stepped down slowly. I watched her bright-white high-heeled shoes as they came in contact with the crumbling bricks of those decaying steps, one by one. Then I imagined how the air surrounding her voluptuous body was permeated by the disgusting smell of the toilet.

The thin, high heels and the enticing legs of that woman stepped down from the steps and onto the bloody paper and string before they passed by me. Even without lifting my head I could see that her breasts didn't quite fit in her shirt, and that her buttons were not all the way buttoned up, revealing white flashes through the collar of her shirt.

When the woman passed, I tried to detect a scent from her, but the way the smell from her body mixed with the smell of the restroom seemed to create a different smell. I tried to remember what this weird smell resembled and finally realized that it smelled kind of like sperm. I was shocked by this feeling because it was not possible for the entire body of a woman to smell like sperm. I turned and looked at the woman as she walked. She seemed to slowly dissolve in the gloom of the fog and disappear.

I didn't even think about asking for directions from that woman as she passed by. Maybe this was because I had just seen her walk out of the restroom or because of the way I was drawn to her form and the feeling of intimidation that came from that. Moreover, the face of this woman was totally without expression. From what I heard from other young men, some women in the big city refuse to laugh due to the worry that their faces will wrinkle. If she didn't laugh around you, it wasn't that she didn't like you, it was just that she was trying to avoid getting wrinkles on her face.

Further away from me there was a white car honking. As if it were honking at me, it attracted my attention. It might have given me this feeling because it was a white color. Once I looked at it, I remembered the old, filthy telephone in my office that was always ringing, like the voice of a sick man who has a problem with his respiratory system. I remembered it because the number on the license plate of the car was exactly the same as the last four digits of that telephone in my office.

I would have really liked to give my office phone number to others, but no one in the city had ever asked me for my phone number. Sometimes I wrote this number on a paper and then sometimes read the numbers from left to right and then from right to left. Sometimes I added the numbers together and sometimes multiplied them. Finally, I would take the second digit and multiply it by the power of the first digit, add it to the third digit multiplied by of the root of the fourth digit, and then adding the sum of these numbers to the fifth digit, I would get the birthday of our neighbor's daughter. Once I realized this, it seemed as though the lights in the office shifted into a faintly bluish color. The identical sequence of those numbers and the birthday of our neighbor's dark-skinned daughter felt like a sign of something mysterious.

The skin of our neighbor's daughter was dark hued. Her skin seemed to glow darker under the sun on the wasteland. From further away the wasteland seemed to be absolutely empty, but when you got closer you could see that there was scrubby grass covering everything. The grass growing in this hard marshland was like the people of this place: stout, dry, and very firm. If you looked at the dark green grass you might think that it was as soft as grass in other places, but if you sit on it, the tips of the blades of the grass would prick you even though they didn't have any thorns. We sat together in a pit in the ground. I'm not sure if this hole was left over from a dried-out spring or if it was dug out by someone else. They might have dug it to get water. The soil was already turned over so there wasn't any prickly grass. I had sat close to her, and wanted to sit even closer still, but I didn't move closer and just waited for her to sit closer to me. The suffocatingly hot weather choked my breath. There seemed to be more than just one sun burning the universe; instead it seemed that the bright blue sky itself was spiting fire into the ground. The shadow of the mud pile wasn't enough to cover where we were sitting in the hole. The whole earth seemed to be radiating with extreme heat. Wanting to whisper in my ear, she moved closer to me, making me feel the heat of her sweating body. Her breath warmed my face and touched me like fire. It was as if she didn't want her heat to escape without making me uncomfortable, so she cupped her hands and whispered in my ear. The skin of her hands was callused from uprooting weeds from the ground every day. They were stained with the pigments of the weeds. The smell of the weeds was grafted onto her hands forever. The smell of her hands was like that light, wet smell of newly cut weeds. This kind of smell wasn't just in her hands but embedded in her whole body. On her dripping sweaty body, there was no smell of sweat but rather always the smell of weeds. Even when she took her hand away from my face as she talked, I sensed the smell of the weeds on her breath.

She asked me whether or not I remembered something. I wasn't exactly sure what thing she was talking about. She repeated her initial question. I told her I didn't remember. She was surprised that I didn't even remember that kind of thing. It would be unimaginable for her to forget it. She asked me why I forgot it. Can I, a man, remember things that haven't happened?

When I said this out loud to her, her attention was somewhere else, and I realized that she hadn't wanted to hear my answer when she asked me this question. She looked at me afterward, but the light of her eyes didn't come to me, and she instead stared into vacant space. At this moment it seemed as though she was concentrating all of her attention on herself. As though she was moving into sexual bliss, she sank into the senses of her own body. It was as if she totally separated herself from the world.

I gazed at the piled-up clouds in the sky. I surprised myself with the thought that I could see the clouds as letters and add them together. Since then, whenever I lay on the edge of a field, I would add the clouds together and read them. Later when I told this to our neighbor's daughter, she made fun of me for exactly two months. Since then, whenever I lay together with her in the desert, I looked at the sky secretly and avoided telling her that I was reading the clouds. While she thought I was looking at her body, actually my eyes stayed focused on the sky.

The small particles of the fog kept hitting my face with their icy cold substance. By then I felt that my face was becoming red like the face of a very sick person. Then I came back to my body from the fog, concentrating my attention into my body's interior. My stomach, as if full of fog, lost some sensation and became very tense. On the one hand, it wouldn't be satiated even after swallowing the whole world. But on the other hand, it didn't have space for anything else. My body was warm, but the blood in my veins seemed to be moving very slowly, as if it would gradually stop and solidify as ice. It was as if the icy water particles hitting my face, in contrast to the heat in my body, stopped me from feeling my pulse. Instead it felt like my blood flow had been halted, clogged by some floating debris. My brain felt empty, like a house after it had been robbed. I would have liked it if my brain stayed like this. When my brain is empty, I feel very relaxed. At these times, my brain doesn't function at all. I can't think through the simplest of things. Although this relaxation and enjoyable stupidness is just momentary, and although it is a sign of an endless flood of painful feelings to come, I always like this disembodied condition.

The fog gradually became thicker until it seemed to be transformed from a gas into a fluid. I imagined myself floating in that fluid. Suffocating in it. Suddenly I felt as though I was suffocating, as though I was short of breath. When I walked into an intersection of the back streets, I got over the feeling of air hunger, as though the intersection of the streets gave me some sort of freedom to choose. The choice to walk along any of the four streets was my freedom, but this freedom itself left me confused.

I hesitated at the intersection for a while, deciding which road to walk along. Although the wood shutters of the bottle shop were closed and fastened by a big iron rod, a light could still be seen through them. The crack of gloomy light between the two wood shutters was like a long wound that had been cut by a knife and together with the fog made the intersection seem horrible and made me shudder.

I imagined the way the bottle shop must be full of the scent of sorghum liquor.*

Before I came to the city, I had always imagined that because of all the candy stores, the big city must be filled with the scent of candy. Although I had not been to the city, the thought of the sweet taste and scent of the candy made me imagine mysterious and enticingly strange abstract visions of the city. Because the city in my imagination was a virtual thing shaped by a combination of unachievable perfection and an unceasing assault on my senses, the virtual city in my imagination could not be realized in a tangible form. The city of my imagination wouldn't allow me to capture it. Instead, it always vanished and reappeared in a new form. The only thing that remained consistent was the scent of the candy. Perhaps this was because I knew about candy that came from that distant, mysterious city. During Eid al-Adha and Eid al-Fitr, our guests would sometimes unexpectedly give us one or two candies. Those candies would make me feel the illusion that this city really existed.

Perhaps because my father was gone, my house seemed bigger. The spaciousness of the house allowed me to sleep sweetly. In my dreams, the thunderous sound of a storm became indistinguishable from a giant bonfire. I danced the *sama* in a circle around the fire. The sound of it formed the rhythm of this Sufi dance. At that moment it was as if the cackling voice of a female shaman was cursing my name in the distance. The sound gradually got closer and suddenly made everything in front of my

---

* Sorghum liquor is a standard spirit associated with Han Chinese culture. Since the 1990s, it has been a widespread source of alcoholism among less pious Muslim Uyghurs. Since 2017, when the mass internment of Uyghurs began, abstaining from alcohol has been deemed a sign of religious extremism.

eyes disappear, bringing me back to that frayed, threadbare felt mat. As if it was an expression of her five organs, I would see my mother's fixed look of confusion, worry, and helplessness. It made her face appear permanently creased with gloom and age.

My mother always took me on long walks along the dark streets searching for my father. The sound that the front of my mother's dress would make while flapping in the wind reminded me of the sound of the flames of the bonfire in my dreams.

We worried that my father would get drunk and stumble into the irrigation channels, so we looked in each of the ditches and under the bridges one by one. Finally, we would end up in one of those establishments filled with the strong scent of candy. Although the fragrance was strong enough to make my throat sore, I still sniffed at the air desperately, breathing it deeply into my lungs, not noticing anything else. My father was among these odd-faced people, his eyes very red, his nose thin and long, the space between his eyebrows and the hair on his head almost connected on his forehead, his eyes very scary, his skin like copper.

When one drunk saw us he scowled and glared at us with an eye that had a black spot in the white part of it. All of them glared at us with their red eyes. I saw one person whose face seemed unforgettably ugly. There weren't any blemishes on his face, and to this day I don't know why he looked so ugly. Although a lot of time has passed since then, and at that time everyone's face looked as though it had changed its shape in an exaggerated way, I still can't help but think that that face was the strangest. His baggy lower eyelids were a bluish color as though they intentionally wanted to embarrass him. Later I heard from others that he had a kidney disease. One of these people had a scarred chin that quivered in a very frightening way.

I'm not sure whether that scene was a true scene from when my mother and I were looking for my father or if I just made it up by imagining it over and over until it became stable in my brain, and I thought I could actually see it in reality.

My feelings of fear in the big city perhaps came from the influence of my childhood experience of that strong smell of candy, my father, and the faces of those strange and nervous people who were seared in my mind. Although I had never been to the big city, for a long time my imagination of it was based on those smells and faces. The desire for the sweet smell of the candy and the feeling of fear those strange faces produced a contradictory psyche that was both attracted and repulsed. And because of this, I would sink into unending loneliness, mysterious anxiety, and irrational sadness.

At that time, I didn't really know what the smell was like at liquor gatherings. Many years later, my own wide shoulders and elongated face that came from my father appeared among the drunken faces and the thick smoke of cigarettes. It was then that I realized that the smell was not from candy, but the smell of alcohol on their breath.

I used to think that the mentality of fear in the big city was mostly due to the threat of being lost that people there faced. Before I saw the city, the city in my imagination was as infinite as the desert outside of our village. Just as there were village boys who spread unexplainable, strange rumors about the desert, there were also mysterious, horrible myths that spread about the big city. The only difference between these myths was that they had different characters. The main characters in the myths about the desert were angels and demons, but in myths about the city the main characters were women. Being lost was the main theme of these myths.

One night I was lost in the desert. The darkness made the desert infinite. In the midst of that infinity a hesitant, unmoving little body became transfixed with fear. That seven- or

eight-year-old kid was me. No matter where I looked, everything seemed to be the same. There was nothing that could
give me a sense of direction. The blankness of everything in the
darkness made a person imagine that there was an infinite possibility for things to exist. The thing that frightened me was this
infinity—because in this infinity there were more things that
I couldn't imagine than that I could.

Later, I realized that the root of the fears that humans
have is just this: infinity. The infinity of the sky, of time, of not
knowing what comes after death, threatens humans. To eradicate the threat that comes from the infinity of the universe,
humans have broken it up into the small parts where they
live—giving it borders and standards. In order to eradicate the
threat that comes from the infinity of time, they have broken
it up into parts like hours, days, and months, giving it limits.
In order to give a limit to the things confined to the afterlife,
they draw the floor designs and maps of another world. The
reason people fear darkness is because the limits of objects—
the dimensions and volume of individual things—are totally
subsumed in darkness and become a single infinity. The darkness made the horizon of the desert disappear, which frightened me. I didn't know what kind of horrible thing might
suddenly step out of the darkness, but it seemed like a strange,
unimaginable thing might attack me at any time. The form of
the thing that might suddenly emerge was also infinite. I was
unable to imagine how much I would fear that thing, because
there was no tangible shape to the thing that could limit my
imagination.

In the frightening darkness only the stars that were twinkling
at an infinite distance gave the kid, who was overwhelmed by
fear, a sense of familiarity and recognition with which to try
to slightly alleviate his fears. That kid, who was me, had heard

from his peers in the neighborhood about how their fathers had told them how to know the direction by looking at the stars. My father was not the kind of person who ever noticed the things that existed in our natural surroundings. It was hard for me to know whether he knew stars existed in the sky or not. I didn't believe that my father had ever looked at them.

In that desert night when I couldn't decide which way to walk, I searched the stars for a while. The stars hung silently in the sky. I wanted to find my way by looking at them, but I couldn't make any sum out of them. The stars were very far away and cold. They seemed not to give me a sense of anything. My body was cold with fear and my heart was beating hopelessly as I looked at the stars for a while. Suddenly one star left its place, crossed the deepest parts of the sky, and disappeared in the darkness. From this it seemed that the star was guiding me, telling me which direction to go. I followed the path of the star and began walking. After walking a while, I wanted to know whether my path was correct or if unknowingly I had turned in the wrong direction, so I stopped and looked at the stars in the sky again. Then another shooting star crossed the sky. I kept walking, following the path of that star. In this way, I continued to walk along the path of the falling stars.

After this, for a long time I always thought that the reason the stars fell in the desert sky was in order to give direction to those lost in the darkness. Then one day my mother told me that a star falling in the sky was a sign that someone had died and taught me a verse to recite when I saw them fall. But I still couldn't change my belief that the reason stars fell was to give direction to the lost.

As I floated up and sank into the fog as I walked, I began to realize that the fog was similar to the shadows. I realized that just as the exact shape of the darkness is shadows, the exact shape of fog is disappearance. The exact shape of humans is also disappearance. At this moment I felt as though my body was transforming into the final stage of humanity.

After I came to the city, I felt as though the threat of getting lost and the desire to lose myself were strangely becoming one inside me. Although everything in the distant and powerful city, Beijing, where I spent my five years of college, felt strange to me. And even though the tall buildings, wide roads, and the ditches and canals were built according to a grid of the same standard and shape so that it wasn't easy to differentiate one from another, I never had the feeling of being lost. Every person in that city felt like one person. All of them were folded into each other. Their faces, voices, and gestures were tied firmly to each other like the matted hair of a Uyghur shaman. Moreover, to us boys, the men and women seemed to be identical. You could only tell them apart by stripping off their clothes and taking a look. The faces of the men were beardless like women and their skin was very delicate and unadorned. I was always surprised by how they could tell each other apart. Later I realized that it wasn't just me. Many other people had the same problem differentiating people of the same ethnicity from each other, even people from the city.

Often, we went to watch the only TV on campus, in the corridor of a building where the old cadres stayed when they came to continue their education. Us Uyghurs who came to improve our knowledge in the city always argued about whether or not the person who had done something unusual earlier in the TV show was the same person that we saw now. We would argue about this from the beginning to the end of the show. Other people who couldn't stand this sort of endless arguing would leave the TV to us and go. At first when classes began, we couldn't tell the difference between teachers, though gradually we were able to tell men and women apart, and eventually we could even tell our teachers apart. But the other people in the city always stayed more or less identical to us. Later, the most surprising thing to me was that the people in the city could never differentiate us from each other either. One time a couple of police, who came looking for some people who had broken some windows during a fight at a restaurant and then run away, ordered us to stand in line and asked the restaurant owner to look at us and identify who the culprit was. He couldn't tell who it was even though he looked at us very carefully. He said we all look so much like each other that it was impossible to tell us apart. He sighed heavily and left.

At this moment, I stood on the corner of the back streets of the city that was surrounded by fog, hesitating about which way to go. At the entrance of each of the four streets there were no street names or any sign of what place this was.

After the big city appeared before my eyes in tangible form, the infinite variability of the city from my childhood imagination seemed to have been secured by the limits of reality, but, nevertheless, for a long time I couldn't get over the threat that came from the infinity of my imagination. The source of the feeling of inexplicable sadness that came from the big city might be this.

While I was standing there at the intersection of the streets, the numbers were rushing through my brain. The district numbers, zip codes, phone numbers, residential area numbers, building numbers, house numbers, the years, months, and dates, the hours, minutes and seconds, ID numbers, page numbers of books, passwords, and the numbers that are held in secret and represent people, and the people who represent those numbers. . . .

There were no buildings on this topsy-turvy winding street, just single-story houses.* But the sense of the city it gave a person was heavier and fuller than the big streets full of tall buildings. The relationship between these houses and the numbers of the city was much more mystical and mysterious.

I had majored in math in college. I always stopped at the library after class since my math classes didn't satisfy my abnormal desire for numbers. I searched endlessly through all the books about numbers. As if they were words and my thoughts were melting, my thoughts flowed among the numbers. My life in that distant, cold city only existed inside the four corners of the dormitory, cafeteria, classroom, and library. My roommates in the dormitory were afraid that a person who read a lot of books would go crazy. They wouldn't go to the library and instead just sat in the cramped, filthy dorm room that smelled of shoes and socks. That smell would fill their inner organs and cause them to look at each other with anger and resentment. When I walked out of the library and back to the dorm, lost among the numbers bursting in my brain, it seemed as though I could hear the sound of my roommates' teeth and necks. They always had insulting words ready for me, because it seemed to them that I had occupied an additional corner that had previously belonged to them. It may have been to take the place of what they had done in that corner that every Sunday when the buses were jammed, they would take a random bus and stand behind strange-smelling women who had different skin and press up against them.

---

* Here the author is describing the "shantytowns" where many Uyghurs lived on the margins of Ürümchi, prior to 2009 and the large scale "urban renewal" demolition projects. These projects, along with the People's War on Terror, which began in 2014 and produced a passbook and checkpoint system, banished many Uyghurs from the city.

When they got back to the dorm they would tell their stories of how they had pressed up against them. How those women had responded. How their hard-ons had bulged out.

Before I went to the city, I only knew about some of the famous palaces, squares, and gates. I had seen a picture that had represented the inhabitants of the city as a mass of tiny little lines. But after I arrived, my knowledge of the city retracted to less than when I had been living several thousand kilometers away. I felt as if that city was actually growing further and further away from me. When a teacher in an empty classroom said that a change in a numerical amount would result in a change in quality, I imagined that this number might be a soul and that this quality might be a body. This description of the relationship between changing numbers and changes in quality gave me a sign of how changing the soul would affect changes in the body. The changes in the body that came from a lustful imagination were the proof of this. Following this logic, I imagined that the face of a person who was full of evil thoughts would gradually become uglier and that his legs would become twisted.

I also felt as though the countless numbers stuck in my brain were making my face glow. Although my classmates always said that my face was ugly, I felt like I was becoming better and better looking. As I walked out of the library with my brain full of numbers, I felt like I was the best-looking person in the world.

In the office, I opened the drawer. To shield it from the view of my colleagues, I hid it with the hem of my jacket as if I were protecting the purity of a virgin. I looked at the numbers one by one and began guessing their meanings. I was both excited and frightened by my desire for those numbers.

There were several digits written on every line of the paper. The number on the first line had a relationship to me. The number on the second line was a five-digit number. I thought this

must be a telephone number. But when I tried to dial it, I found
out that no number like that existed. The nonexistent number
swallowed me and held me in the dark embrace of its under-
world. I thought I hadn't dialed the number right, so I tried
again. But it still came back as nonexistent. Immediately I dialed
the numbers starting from right to left. This time, before I could
even finish dialing half of the numbers, the message that results
from a misdialed number came from the telephone. I'm not
sure why, but I found the message contained in this nonexistent
number exciting. I could not resist putting my fingers into the
dial of the telephone and turning it again. Of course, no matter how many times I tried to dial it, the result never seemed
to change. Maybe this wasn't a telephone number after all, but
rather some other kind of number, I thought. The less I knew
about them, the more significant those numbers became to me.
It might have been a number on a public bus. The first two digits
of the number was the route number of the bus that stopped in
front of my office building. To figure out what the final digits
signified, I picked up a city telephone book that was hanging on
a string next to the telephone. Inside the front page there was a
route map for city buses. I started looking at the routes and route
numbers of the buses. The inner pages of the telephone book
were already dirty and the outer pages already faded.

Every time I saw some sort of number, I couldn't walk away
until I had forcefully memorized that number and it was stuck
in my mind. Perhaps this was because my father thought every
subject other than math was worthless and forced me to learn
it alone. He always made me calculate numbers in my mind. To
this day I can't understand why my father had such a desire for
numbers. I didn't believe that he felt that watching the mysterious, infinite flux between numbers might provide him with some
knowledge of the secret, sacred force that was the source of the

universe. But my father's veneration of numbers was very clear. Once, I got sick after eating a tomato. After that, every time I saw a tomato my stomach would turn. In the same way, every time I saw a number my stomach would turn, the rotten smell of millet cakes would burst out of my mouth and up through my nose. It wasn't until after a stronger sensation would smother that feeling that I could look at numbers again. The only things that could do this were feelings of threat and fear. I'm not sure when and how those feelings disappeared, but later those feelings were totally reversed. Suddenly I felt as though I could face numbers without waiting for some grim threat to burst through my body and scare me sober. Because I had always seen my father's angry face in my mind's eye when I was young, I hadn't known how to face numbers without this sort of threat. When my hatred toward numbers was transformed into an extraordinary desire, the feeling of threat also totally shifted. My body, which had been tamed by terror, became very sensitive to feelings of threat after I left my village.

Numbers weren't only of essential significance for the universe, but also of essential significance for me.

As I stood at the corner, I heard the sound of a door being opened and shut somewhere in the distance. I couldn't tell where this sound was coming from, but as I looked here and there, the figure of a short, fat man appeared in the fog like a dead fish bobbing in the water. He rushed through a line from a folk song in a low voice. From the way he sang, it seemed as though he wasn't following the original tune. From this it seemed clear that the distance he was planning to walk was quite short.* As he

---

* Some rural-origin Uyghurs measure space by the time it takes to sing songs while walking.

got closer to me, I wanted to ask him about my search for the street on which the building number 6891 was located. But once I opened my mouth and spoke the first letter of that street aloud, he stood stock-still and shook as though he had been stabbed in the back with a very sharp knife. He stared at me with anxious, fixed eyes. Perhaps since I had started the word awkwardly and received this sort of shocked response, I couldn't continue what I was saying. So I also just stood there frozen in place.

It was as though both of us were standing in the thick fog of the darkness and his shocked look was a condition of the time, but I saw that miscreant's flattened face and owl-like eyes as if he had been standing in front of me for several hours. The weird expression on his face was something I had never seen before on the faces of others.

After that he walked very quickly, as if he were halfway running, and went into a walled residential area off to the side of the street. I was just standing there like I was made of stone, fixed in place. I just couldn't understand why he was so shocked. It couldn't be because of my appearance, because apart from the anxiety in my eyes and shocked expression on my face, my appearance was actually more cordial than most. I knew I didn't look like a thief or a cruel criminal. On top of this, I had treated him in a very reserved and polite way. I thought perhaps he might be a migrant. But it seemed like he lived on this street. If this hadn't been the case, he wouldn't have been able to walk out of one house and immediately walk into another.

I looked for a while at the side of the street where he had disappeared. After a bit, I began to feel like he might wonder why I had asked directions and bring out a bunch of people to beat me. I immediately turned toward the street in front of me and began to walk. The fog in this street was the same. The back streets of the city were becoming dimmer and dimmer, like the feeling of a body that was being beaten to death. The fog was submerging every part of it, sinking it into unconsciousness. As if I were the last living cell in that body, I walked sluggishly. I felt I was experiencing how this city slowly froze in place and the last bit of warmth in its body was slowly snuffed out. I tried to sense the last faint shudder in this delicate body, but I couldn't feel it. I wished that I could flutter away from this dark back street with that last final breath. But the kind of courage that only belongs to losers, and the bravery that only belongs to the depressed, seemed to lead me not toward this exit, but toward the center of the darkness and fog.

After the first few days I spent in the city, the weather had never been clear, so I didn't know from which side the sun rose or on which it set. The only thing that gave me a sense of direction was the only thing that belonged to me in this city—the drawer in the office. All of my belongings were in that drawer, so no matter where I went in the city, that drawer would attract me to it with the pull of an invisible string. No matter where I stood if I wanted to go somewhere, I would measure how far away it was based on its distance from the drawer in that office.

The smiling-faced person in my office told me that the office would offer me a whole desk, but the things in the other drawers in it belonged to a person who had retired eleven years before. Because this person still hadn't retrieved his belongings from the drawers, there was no possibility that they might be emptied for me. He always spoke in an astonishingly intimate manner. If you saw his pleasant demeanor, you would think that no one in the world could dislike him—especially the women in this big city. "How could a person have such a nice personality?" I thought sometimes. Later I was surprised to find out that no one in the office liked him. I don't know why they didn't like him. Perhaps they were annoyed because the skin on his face always shone very whitely, as if it had been polished. Perhaps they were also annoyed because his long, thin figure was like a dancer's, and he strode in a very smooth and orderly way, as if he were measuring each step.

When there was no one in the office, with gratitude and passion, as if I were looking at the body of a woman for the first time, I always very carefully examined that desk that offered me that one drawer. It was as though I knew that this secretly watched woman did not fully belong to me and that I couldn't fully possess any other part of her. I could only look. But still, I was satisfied with this. I was afraid that someone would see me staring longingly at that desk, so I only looked at it after I had firmly closed the door.

I examined the desk, looking in the drawers and cabinets through small gaps at their edges and trying to see what was inside. But because the gaps were very narrow, and the insides of the drawers were very dark, I couldn't see anything very clearly. In the places closest to the gaps I could vaguely see that there were one or two sheets of paper. I lifted the desk several times to weigh what might be inside. The desk was very light, and I couldn't imagine that there was anything in it other than those old pieces of paper. When I asked him to force the person who had sat at this desk more than ten years ago to empty the desk, the smiling-faced man said the retired person still had not agreed to do so.

I never met that person so I'm not sure why, but in my imagination, he was ill, bedridden, and had loose wrinkled skin on his face. His arms and neck were speckled with black spots like the scales of a fish. If he lost his connection with that desk, it seemed that he might stop breathing. That desk was the only thing that tied him to society, people, and life itself. It was like he had used all of his strength to hang on to this over the past ten years. After I came to this realization, I didn't even want to own all of the desk. His identity was assured only by that desk. The only thing that could prove to him that he had once been a worker in this city office was that these drawers were locked in the dim, dank part of this office building. Apart from this desk he would be nothing. He didn't even know what kind of person he was, what his name was or how old he was. Without his connection to the desk, he would just be a substance that could be discarded, lying on some bed in a corner of the house. Trash that could be thrown away in a few days. Nothing more than a piece of rotting meat.

I felt just like that old man—like a piece of trash before being thrown away—as I walked in the fog. At that moment, as the fog seeped into my body, I felt myself begin to age. I felt my skin gradually loosen, my bones becoming brittle, my eyes becoming cloudy. In order to get over this feeling I used all of my strength to remember that drawer and which side of the desk it was on. But what first appeared in my eyes was that smiling-faced guy who had sat in front of me and how his manner gradually became unbearable. His personality made me squirm.

The other day he found out that I had spent all night in the office sitting in the chair because I had nowhere to stay. I was afraid that other people would find out, so I hadn't turned on the lights. Actually, this wasn't the only reason, I just didn't want to turn them on. I like the darkness more than the fluorescent lights in the office. The lights that were on all day, because there was no sunlight in the office, looked like pale faces desperate for blood—which also made me squirm.

The smiling-faced person criticized me. He warned me not to stay in the office all night again. He said if it happened again, he would kick me out of the office. The angrier he became, the broader the smile on his face became. It made my eyes widen.

Finally, I just couldn't bear his smile anymore, and I walked out of the office into the corridor and stood there for a while.

When I was standing in front of my office, hesitating about which way to go when I took off from work that afternoon, there was a janitor who always had open sores under his nose who kicked me out—not letting me stand there for even a minute. His articulation and use of complex tones were even loftier and more decisive than that smiling-faced man.* His kingly attitude made me even more depressed. I wanted to make him aware that he had no authority to order me about. I could stomp his attitude into the ground. But the decisiveness in his voice made me confused and I entered a state in which I no longer believed that I really had ownership over that drawer. I took on the affect of that rat crossing the street as I left the corridor in front of my office.

The sky of the city has no stars. Even though the weather was so clear during the day, you could never see any stars at night. In my mind, people that look at the stars and recognize some constellations or small points of significance are people with very powerful imaginations. I, on the other hand, was someone who had a weak imagination. Sometimes a sudden strengthening of my imagination would put me into a state of anxiety. I didn't want my brain to remain in the same murky turbid state of being that it was in before the universe was created. Only the dim state of this foggy city gave me a place to rest. I worried that my imagination would suddenly get stronger and my brain would begin to glow. This kind of glowing was as frightening as someone entering the pitch blackness and not being able to distinguish anything. But this cloudiness did not signify an endless state of restfulness, because it was pregnant with everything. It was the

---

* Here the author is indicating that the janitor was a Mandarin speaker.

beginning of a horrible creation. I imagine that the period from the state of murkiness to the beginning of creation must have been perfectly soundless with a kind of creepy suspense and terrible peacefulness.

The murky condition of the city in the fog, the murky mental condition of my brain, and the ambiguous position of my identity in the Xinjiang Uyghur Autonomous Region seemed to be totally of the same substance; sometimes they mirror each other and sometimes they seep into each other. Due to the constant threat of choking from the inside, being smothered or drowning, for most people this peacefulness seemed to be more dangerous than the most frightening panic.

I lost my sense of direction when I first came to the city. Since I was a kid, I've always thought the higher ground was the north and the lower the south, and because of this I always felt disoriented. Even after I realized that my method for determining directions was wrong, I couldn't correct it. My small village was located on the southern slope of the Tian Shan mountains. As you walked to the south, the land gradually descended into a scrubby marshland. When the sheep we were herding were grazing, I would lie in the grass with my head resting toward the north and feel as though it was higher than the rest of my body. This feeling that I got from my birthplace became a permanent principle of my constitution. It grasped me very firmly and prevented me from correctly understanding the geographical situation and cardinal directions of other places.

Ürümchi is located in a narrow valley that looks like the scar of a deep wound. In opposition to the orientation of my village, in this city the water flows from south to north, but in my mind, water should naturally flow toward the south. I couldn't come to terms with the idea of water flowing from south to north. Now, in the fog, my sense of direction was deteriorating even more. I couldn't even judge which direction was higher and which was lower.

I heard the sloshing sound of muddy footsteps as I walked. This noise made me really sad. I didn't know why this sound made me sad. Perhaps it was because it sounded like blood splatting on the ground.

I don't know anyone in this strange city, so it's impossible for me to be friends or enemies with anyone.

It was difficult to determine whether or not the forms on the road were human. As I looked at them I thought, *What time is it? Is it day or night? What day is it?* Suddenly I realized that I couldn't recall any such markers. *What month is this?* Not only this, but I couldn't even remember what year it was. My awareness suddenly seemed to fade out. *What century is it now?* In the end I gradually lost my sense of what era I was a part of. I was lost in time. It began to dawn on me that people could become homeless exiles not only in space but also in time. They can struggle to ascertain where they belong in the infinity of time. Maybe all of us are wandering exiles in time or a simulation of time. Perhaps the original form and standards of time were very different from what they are simulating today. Compared to the original form of time, perhaps the calculations of people to separate it out into days, weeks, months, and years is a kind of children's game. It's like one philosopher said, "If a person tries to make plans, it only makes God laugh." I tried to come to terms with my place in time by joining and accepting the simulated form of time that others had put into practice. But I couldn't even make myself aware of this. Because I'm also human, I felt I had to accept the concept of the time made by other humans and feel comfort in satisfying my desire to know the world my mind belongs to in time. But it seemed as though time had suddenly disappeared and that I was now in a place where time had not been created.

The number on the last line of the paper covered with footprints had four digits. I was looking just at those numbers. The first number of that line was the beginning of every other number. It seemed like it was the beginning of everything and a reflection of everything. This number embraced me and gave me a feeling of infinity, because every other number in the world appeared to be just a derivation of that original number. The second number on that line was the final number out of all numbers. Humans always imagine the end of time as related to that number. This number signifies death and completion. The number that was written on the back side of the paper was exactly the opposite of that number. What it signified was diametrically opposed to it. At first people related it to life, later they thought of it as related to sexual power, and then finally settled on Satan. The last number of that line was a repetition of that second number.

I assumed that the first two digits of the four-digit number were for a certain residential area, and the last two digits indicated a certain house. This number made me go down a back street. It was very narrow and damp. The walls smelled of dank earth. This was the final number I would look for today.

For centuries, this strange desire for numbers has been crawling up through people's heads without cease. To discover the source of the universe, they wanted to unravel the mysterious relationships between different numbers. This desire to know was both forbidden by God, and, at the same time, a source of threat, due to the ineptitude of human intelligence. They were always afraid of being thrown into a fire and burning in punishment. I imagine that the so-called witches of the world who were killed by being thrown into fires were also obsessed with wanting to understand the mysterious relationships between numbers. They wanted to understand the secret schemes of God, and for this reason they were thrown into the flames. For them, being thrown into a fire was like burning the *dadüi* account records immediately after confirming that the higher-ups were coming to check on them.* It was like a small kid who burned a bunch of money thinking it was just a bunch of paper, and how that kid's father stuck the kid's head into an iron stove, killing him. The ultimate cause of this murder of a three-year-old son was numbers.

My father always told me these horrific stories. Like how someone broke his own kid's leg after the kid let a sheep's leg get broken while he was watching them. Or how someone stomped his kid's head into the mud and abandoned him after the kid let a donkey cart get stuck in a swamp. Somehow these things seemed to belong not to the past but to the future. The news featured in magazines also seemed to be a prediction. Every day I opened the magazines that came to our office, and if I saw at a glance a word relating to lung disease, I always felt as though it had been deliberately printed on that paper in order to give me a sign that I would get a lung disease sometime in the near future. Then a deep hopelessness would come over me, making me feel powerless. It made me want to throw myself into the nearest corner and lie there.

People around me were crawling in the fog like they had miserable illnesses. Among them there was only one small kid who

---

* *Dadui* is a Chinese term for "large work brigade," which is the smallest entity of village government in the Chinese Communist Party governance structure.

gave me a different impression. He was clomping along with oversized shoes, trying with all of his might to keep up with the tall man in front of him. I wanted to ask this underdeveloped kid, who appeared to have grown up without enough nutrition because his mother stopped producing milk, for directions, but I found it impossible. Since all he wanted to do was to catch up to the person in front of him, he couldn't stop to answer my questions. Before I could open my mouth, he passed me very quickly. The wind that remained from when he passed me shivered around my body for a while before it gradually became a single substance with the cold fog and vanished. The sight of him dragging his oversized shoes remained for a while in my mind's eye. I carefully listened to the way he had dragged his shoes. I was surprised that I could hear that sound even in the far distance because this didn't fit with reality. Maybe there was another sound that was similar, and I had mixed the two of them together in my mind. The face of the man who was leading the kid had a serious expression, but his footsteps still gave me the impression that he was just as lifeless as everyone else around him.

When I was a village boy, I didn't believe that the day would ever come that I would find clothes that fit. I always wore leftover clothes from my brother. I worried that other people would be able to tell that my clothes were hand-me-downs. Since my clothes were too big, people would always ask me in a malicious way if they were left to me by my father or my brother. The hardest thing about this was the way my family would make me wear my unspeaking sister's old clothes after they were altered a bit. Every time I wore her clothes I felt like I was becoming dumb just like her. It was as though those clothes were too tight to fit her body. Because she had difficulty taking them off, she had to get used to not taking them off. They seemed to press down on her with a lot of pressure and this is what stopped her voice. Sometimes I would hear her say a few words in her sleep. I thought maybe this was because she had taken off her clothes before lying down. So I believed that maybe, if she took off her already faded and ill-fitting clothes, she could talk. Later when I was old enough to go to school and they thought I had grown up and could lie on a sleeping platform by myself, they got rid of me by giving me a separate room and so I never heard my sister make a sound again. In this way I gradually came to doubt the memory. As a boy, it would have been unimaginably horrible if others had noticed I was wearing a girl's clothes. But nobody ever noticed it. Because among my sister's clothes there were very few reddish-colored clothes, my mom only altered the clothes that were male-colored. I always hoped that my sister's next set of clothes would be red, because then my family wouldn't make me wear them. In any case, it was horrifying for me to wear hand-me-downs from a girl. There is a saying I heard all the time that the private parts of a boy who wears girls' clothes will disappear, shrinking smaller and smaller, withdrawing until they look like female private parts. After I began wearing my sister's clothes, I would find places to hide, pull down my pants, and look at them for long periods of time.

When my sister was married off I was happy that I could stop wearing her altered clothes, but later she began bringing me her husband's castoffs. It was very hard for me to wear clothes that smelled like animal diarrhea and a stranger's body. It was as if he laid down and got up in a barn. Even washing them over and over, you couldn't get rid of that kind of smell.

Her eyes always looked uncertain. Her breath smelled like a cold-storage turnip cellar. The dry skin on her firm face was always flaking. Since my sister married very young, she just lived silently with that man who was thirty years her elder, until eventually she ran away with a handyman who worked in their home. Her husband was very skinny with a bald patch on the back of his head that looked different from the skin on the rest of his body. It was as if he was afraid that others wouldn't notice it, so he always turned his collar down very deliberately and rubbed it. It was easy for me to forget about this asshole, who always handed out desert dates from his greasy prayer hat to women passing by on the road. I was very happy that she ran away, even though listening to my father swear, describing from the thread to the needle the way he would kill her if he caught her, made me squirm.

Later my brother also disappeared from home without a trace. We heard that he had taken up with a woman who was forty years older than him and that he lived as an itinerate brick-maker, moving from town to town. He couldn't get away from that woman. Although many people offered to give him their eighteen-year-old daughters in marriage, he wouldn't agree and just continued to follow that woman on and on. Apart from this totally unreliable information and sourceless news, there was nothing to prove that he existed in this world. He seemed to have disappeared forever. His disappearance brought nothing but anger to our family. It meant that we had lost a member of our family's workforce—a loss equal to the loss we suffered one year when one of our donkeys died. The only difference was that when the donkey died, my father didn't talk to anyone for several days, but when my brother left, my father cursed him endlessly. After my brother disappeared his work fell on my shoulders, and I had more of a burden, but I was happy that I didn't have to wear his old clothes.

At this moment, the scent of candy came from somewhere. Even though this smell was mixed with the rotten urine smell of a bathroom, I could still detect it. It might have been from a small kid passing me with candy in his mouth, or perhaps it came from his drool—if he couldn't maintain control over it as he sucked on the candy. Who knows, perhaps it came from someone who was afraid of the smell of a hospital and doused himself with candy-scented cologne. Later when I found out that candies were made from fruits that you could find anywhere, I was really disappointed. In my mind, candy was something that could be made only in some mythical, impenetrable place. It seemed as though it must be made from unimaginable elixirs. There is nothing more wounding than understanding the simplicity of the intricate thing to which one had been so attached before. When I realized this, I felt as though surgery in a hospital must also be as simple as digging through the inner parts of a doll.

As I was contemplating the differences between the building numbers on the doors, I stumbled over a fist-sized stone and tripped. My hand touched the icy cold ground, and something stuck to my palm. After I got up my palms burned as if I had touched an iron stove. I looked around to see if anyone had seen or not. I thought perhaps I would see people laughing, but nothing changed on the fixed faces among the passersby. Their eyes remained trained on their original destination. I remembered that I had passed through the entrance to the street using my right foot. It was actually very clear that I had used my right foot first, but suddenly I began to doubt it. Stumbling over a stone was a sign of past improper steps.

This back street of the city was in the center, far away from the rocky cliffs and hillsides. So this stone seemed to have been intentionally brought here for hitting someone; there could have been no other purpose for it than injuring people. I peered down at it. One side of the stone was wet. It seemed to be a bloodstain. I picked it up and stroked it with my hand. The icy stone made my palms cold. I walked over to a window and looked again at the wetness on my hand in the light. The liquid on my hand that had come from the stone seemed like it might truly be blood. I shivered suddenly, not knowing how to clean my contaminated hand. I looked up at the window and noticed that its curtain was red. Perhaps it was just the light coming through that window curtain that was making the wetness on my hand appear red, which in turn was making me think it might be blood. I took a little breath and walked on to look at it again under the light of a window with differently hued curtains.

Looking carefully at the street, it seemed as though some of the houses were newer than others. The winding disorder of the street would make anyone who looked think that the houses were old and shabby. Actually, some were so new that no number had yet been written on their front doors. The numbers of others were very haphazard. Some of them were written in red paint, others were written in blue paint. Some of them were stamped out of tin. Some were very large, while others were very small. Some of them were written out in characters. It was not difficult to assume that these numbers were written at different periods of time and that every time they were written they became more and more disorderly. Some of them were faded so much that even if you looked really carefully, you couldn't discern what numbers they were. I looked at the mantle of every door and tried to read the numbers or even the traces of the numbers. Some of the numbers were so faded that standing there for such a long time analyzing their meaning felt like doing an archeological study.

Standing there in front of one house might give the impression that the person is observing the surroundings in preparation for robbing or stealing from that house. So I thought that

I needed to avoid looking like I was standing there looking. Even though I looked very carefully at some of those houses, I came away with no results in the end. Some of them looked like the script of some ancient people that was disappearing without a trace. It was impossible to assume what numbers they had referred to. I felt as though I were an explorer on an expedition in an ancient, unending cemetery. It seemed like I was searching not just for a house with a particular number on this street, but also through the epochs of history. It seemed as though that number had never existed anywhere in time or space. The horror that came from this cemetery of other strange peoples and the confusion that came from the fog made me want to leave this place quickly. But I had to find that house. I wanted to find a house that I could rent. I wanted not to see the faces of others or hear the voices of others, but to enjoy the contentment of solitude, if even for only a day.

I'm not sure why I thought they would rent me the house I was searching for, as if someone were waiting for me to come, and turning away many other renters empty-handed. I had the feeling that if I didn't settle it today, there would be no second chance. The imperceptible ice-cold water particles of the fog stung my face.

The sound of something huge and heavy made of tin slamming down from somewhere high reached me. This sound might have come from a construction site that was still in operation somewhere in the distance. It shook through the fog a single time, and then continued on. It was mixed with the sound of a middle school math teacher slamming a desk with an eraser made out of wood and a scrap of a rug. He had noticed that I had been daydreaming and that my attention wasn't focused on the blackboard. At this moment I was adding my student ID number to those of my classmates one by one and thinking about which signs those results would give me. I was trying out every number's meaning. There wasn't any meaning after I assigned a letter to each number and tried to read them. This signified that I wasn't related to those kids and their ID numbers. My relationship to them seemed to be just like what would result from adding meaningless letters together: nothing but meaningless syllables. Like the many sounds from metal, water dripping, and wet wood in the fire, to me, and to each of them, we were all just sounds that would only give a single note and then disappear. At first, I wrote down my ID number after the ID numbers of others. But when that had no meaning, I redid it and wrote down mine in front of theirs. When I wrote my neighbor's daughter's number beside mine, suddenly it read as my birthday.

It was just then that I was surprised by the teacher angrily slamming the desk with the wood back of the eraser, startling us all. In my shock I looked at him and he made me stand up. As I stood up, I saw a key tied in the middle of the braid of our neighbor's daughter's full-bodied, pitch-black hair. Because I couldn't answer the questions the teacher asked, he made me walk to the front of the class and stand there. I stood there until the end of class. I was forced to stand there with my head bowed. From time to time I stole secret glances over at her. But she was focused on the class and didn't seem to notice me. I was still busy adding her student number to mine in my head. The most surprising thing to me was that as I put my number in front of hers, this time it read as her birthday. This was another beginning to my eternal wandering among numbers.

Just then I passed over a dim line on the road with my left foot and immediately, a feeling of threat welled up inside me. I quickened my steps, wanting to find another line to pass over with my right foot. But it suddenly seemed as though there were no lines anywhere on the road. What was the line I had crossed with my left foot? I looked back and not only the lines but everything seemed to have disappeared in the fog. It felt like the bottom had dropped out and as though I wasn't coming from the other end of the street but rather from infinite nothingness.

I looked for the numbers in front of other people's doors, standing there for a long time without anyone talking to me. I felt guilty for standing there without permission. I couldn't get over this guilt because it felt as if I were looking furtively at their nakedness. Since this place was a road, no one had any right to object if someone were standing there for a long time. I said this to myself, trying to banish the fear in my heart and steel my resolve. I just couldn't get over these worries. There was no common-sense rule about whether someone stands there or not, but the purpose of the road was not that of standing, but rather directly related to walking. In any case, everyone knows that each part of the road belongs to the families whose houses face it. For us, if you speak about the "front door" of a home, it is clear that you are referring to the owner of the home. If you don't include the owner's name, the door doesn't really exist in reality—it becomes an abstract concept.

I stopped in front of a creaky wooden door whose slates were falling apart. The color of the door was probably blue, but since it was so old, it had faded to a light gray color. I suppose it could have been green before, because once upon a time people thought that green was an indication of spring and fertility. They thought that this desire might become true in reality through artifice—so people painted their doors and window frames green, one after another. But a painted thing had no relationship with the crops. If green remains in the fields, it does indicate spring and fertility, but if other things remain green, they signify death and decay. To me this sort of green door seemed to have given in to death and interior decay and thus become very blue. Were I to jump through it, I felt like I would be entering into a time of savagery.

The number on the door was written in two different ways. One was quite faded and seemed to have been written a long time before, while the other was painted with a kind of flawed paint that distorted the original shape of the numbers. Thus it was very difficult to read both of them. The initial number consisted of three digits. I didn't read it because the digits of the number were too few. It was not difficult to guess that the number had been written before there were many houses on this street. The next number was four digits long. The first and last digits were relatively clear, but it was hard to discern the middle two digits. I tried to imagine myself as the writer of the number and wrote those two numbers in my imagination. I tried to surmise from the flowing directions of the paint what the numbers might be, but just at that moment the door opened. The door opener was a woman. When she saw me as she came out, she screamed, dropping the things in her hands, and ran back inside. The things she threw so quickly might have been porcelain bowls, which shattered when she dropped them. A cursing voice and other alarmed voices asking what had happened rose from inside of the house. I snapped back to consciousness and walked away with quick steps. I saw the bulging veins that accompany an angered man's voice in my mind's eye. After a few steps, I thought that even if they were to run after me, they couldn't single me out from among all of the people who were passing this way and that, so I slowed my pace. On top of this, if I walked faster, they could perhaps more easily realize that it was me.

The fog spread through my shivering body like a feeling of fright.

Since I walked with an extremely quick pace, I very quickly came to a main road. I thought perhaps I had turned onto that previous back street in error, so to confirm that this was the place I was trying to find I looked around for a sign. At the intersection there were no road or store signs to indicate the name of the place.

The sound of the cars on the road was spreading through my nerves again. Every time I walked out onto the main streets, this noise seemed too strong, but suddenly it felt very peaceful. It was like when you mix equal amounts of all of the colors together and they all become gray. If all of the sounds were mixed together in the same way, it might be quite peaceful as well. After this, though, I started to feel the horrible silence that comes from a road filled with the intense sound of cars. At the same time, I started to hear a drawn-out scream. When I left for the city, not long after the car started moving, I sensed a voice calling out to me in the sound of the engine. I asked the reluctant driver to stop the car and I got out and looked around. I could see only the paved road stretching into the distance. There were no humans or demons in the desert. After this I knew that this voice didn't exist, but I couldn't stop being tempted to look for the source when I heard it.

That sound that brought on a feeling of threat and crisis, like the revelation of an irreducible number, revealed a mysterious force. I couldn't reveal the existence of that number to anyone. Just as mystics don't reveal their discoveries to innocents. I would be killed, just as the Persian mystic Bastam or the Greek philosopher Hippasus were destroyed for revealing their discoveries. That sound called to me unceasingly, but I pretended not to hear it. Even though I was listening to it with intense concentration, I couldn't tell exactly what the sound was. The more I focused the more it seemed to be dividing and mixing into different sounds, transmuting, and then vanishing. This might have been because I wasn't hiding what that sound was from others, but rather from myself.

A poisonous light spread from the headlights of the cars. The windows of the buildings shone coldly, emitting a bluish light just like the bluish light in the eyes of a man before he reveals his deception. The various colored lights that hung in the buildings and the various bright store signs were lit intermittently like wounds that would not heal.

I crossed to the other side of the road and looked down the street. There was one road sign at that street corner. It seemed to be floating in the fog like a mirage. I looked at the sign and realized that this wasn't the street of the house I was searching for. Because this street was wider, and the entrance of the street was more diagonal than the street I had come from. It was as if at that moment the fog was making the entrance of the street appear distant and its direction inverted. After I looked around for a while, I came to the conclusion that the street I had been wandering on earlier might actually be the street I was looking for. I decided to have a look at it again.

I realized then that as I had walked here from the office, the mystery of the numbers had taken me over. I wasn't just walking. I was also doing my part in the human history of counting while waiting for something.

The dimly lit liver color of a car slowly moving by was interrupted by something. It had changed color by the time I saw it a second time. I felt like this was a sign for me to go back the way I had come. I stood there looking for the entrance to that diagonal street for a while. I started counting the dimly seen shadows of people moving in that direction. I decided that if the ninth person to pass me were a man then I would turn back. If it were a woman, I would continue on. When the ninth person walked closer it turned out to be an old man.

I went back down the street. There was no place for me to spend the night. As I turned around, I felt as though this street was swallowing people like a desperate womb.

I don't know anyone in this strange city, so it's impossible for me to be friends or enemies with anyone.

At first glance it appeared as though this famous back street of the city was like an abandoned money bag on the road: it both attracts attention and disappoints.

That city where I had studied hadn't become my new living environment. I couldn't participate in that society. I felt as though Beijing were very far away from me, even as I was standing in the middle of it. It felt even further away than when I was living in the village. Maybe this was because so many mysterious and strange myths about it had entered my ears. And these myths made the city seem more and more imaginary—distancing me even more. After us Uyghurs went to that place, our understanding of that city became less than when we were living several thousand kilometers away and only saw propaganda and sketches of building construction drawn with a bunch of lines on the walls and blackboards. The smiling man in my office often asked why I didn't speak his language perfectly, since I had gone to college in Inner China. Our life in college was spent solely in the dormitory, classrooms, and cafeteria. Compared to others, I had one additional destination: the library. We never had any way of practicing the language of the city while we were there. For us, the strange people in the city weren't much different than the trees by the road. The only difference was that unlike the trees, they moved around.

After graduation, I felt that the countryside was rigid and uncomfortably peaceful and that the alluring anxieties of the city were attractive, but I hadn't told anyone about my decision to choose the city in the end. I didn't say goodbye to anyone, no one saw me off and no one welcomed me. Beijing stopped existing for me and instead stood behind me like a cold stage set for those five years, totally wrenched from my memory. I decided not to go to the place where I was supposed to go according to my registration paper—my reporting-for-duty paper or whatever you want to call it. I thought that my desperation to escape from that village came from my desire for the luxuries of the big city. But actually, my desperation to escape was just the urge to escape my memories.

When I came to Ürümchi, I not only felt like it was big, but I also felt like I was really arriving in the big city for the first time. Maybe this was just an exaggeration. Everything is exaggerated here. The existence of numbers was unrelated to the human need to calculate. In the same way the exaggerated condition of the city and its existence itself had no relation to my need to live in it or not. It existed outside of my soul, body, and conception of self. Here, people exaggerated everything infinitely just by the way they lived.

The fog was moving like the sea. If one compares the blood in a human body to the infinite depths of the sea, the former is quite small. But in people's minds the imagery of a sea of blood nevertheless exists. Actually, if you gather the people around the world together and kill them all, their blood wouldn't come close to forming a sea. There is at most two or three kilos of blood in each person. People try to imagine blood like an outrageously seething sea. This might be a sign that their brains have lost control in their desperate desire to let their own blood flow or spill the blood of others.

At this moment, the city surrounded by the dense fog looked like a huge communal shower room. People were naked, ruthlessly suspicious, looking at everyone as if they were the enemy—even the fog couldn't cover the feelings of these people. The expressions that appeared on people's faces in the shower weren't the lust that came from nudity, but rather that which came from the desire to kill another person. When they see other people's naked bodies, they imagine the enjoyment they would receive from seeing what would happen if bullets or knives penetrated those pale, white, tremulous forms. Seeing the way blood spurts out and spreads like a red flag gives them a stronger sense of satisfaction than sex. Because of this, the faces of people in the bathroom are expressionless as they sink into the contemplation of the greatest way of killing other people. There are no other thoughts in their brains. Others take their kids with them into the shower room. They want to raise their kids to be just like themselves, but the kids aren't interested in other things at all and just sneak looks at the sex parts of adults with curiosity and desire. Because of this they grow up prematurely.

Someone who accompanied me on my way to this city told me a story about something he had seen. He said that in a big city some guy brought his seven- or eight-year-old daughter to the men's public shower. Another acquaintance in the bathroom told this guy that this wasn't right. He replied that the girl was still small and didn't understand anything. Using this excuse, he took her into the presence of hundreds of naked men. Actually, if she did understand that it was inappropriate, she would have only felt ashamed, but if she didn't know that she should have a weird feeling, she might accept it as the natural order of things, and it might distort her understanding of sexuality. After hearing this, a vague feeling of horror about the big city passed through my mind.

While I was walking in this narrow backstreet, I came to understand why people madly resented the city. Many times, cities have been destroyed in history, even the most luxurious cities. The animosity toward cities has a long history. There are classic examples of this even in recent times. For example, a leader called Pol Pot in a country in Southeast Asia herded the country's urbanites to the countryside because he thought that city living would ruin their mentality. In those places even the intellectuals were afraid of being ruined by city life, so they rushed to the countryside. This doesn't mean that those who destroyed the city disliked the city, but rather that their love for the city had become unbearable. The luxuriousness of the city made them nervous and made their eyes go blind. It was like when a boy gets the instinct to kill when he looks at a half-naked woman's body and realizes that there is no possibility of possessing it. The desire to destroy is actually a mutation of the desire for sex.

On a thickly rolled cigarette butt that was lying on the ground, one could see the wetness that remained from the lips of a man who had sucked on it with all of his strength. I picked the cigarette butt up in order to feel it. But what I had imagined was incorrect and it was dry. I looked at it carefully and imagined the way the nicotine in the smoke of the cigarette spread through the veins and slowly seeped into the skin through the tiny capillaries, making it black and filthy, transforming a person's face in an extremely wretched way. My dad's face had turned the color of this smoke. It seemed as though he himself would become a bunch of smoke and would float away like fluff in front of my eyes. My mom thought that he would eventually die from lung cancer. But he didn't die from lung cancer; he died instead from liver disease.

At first, in my imagination, the color of the fog seemed to be a reddish color like a poison gas. It seemed as if a person who sucked in this fog would slowly be poisoned. He would gasp for breath, gradually become very weak in his hands and feet, and eventually collapse. In fact, a person wouldn't be immediately poisoned by the fog. Maybe this kind of feeling was just a distorted form of the threat that came from the fear of the city or came from an image derived from the media about saving the environment. Some people seemed to think that all of the changes of the world, with the exception of the deaths of humans, would result in the destruction of the planet.

I thought about why I came to the conclusion regarding the poisonous character of the fog from its reddish tint. Where had I seen this reddish gaseous substance before? Maybe I had seen it in the smoke of a coal-burning stove when I was a kid. Maybe I had also seen that kind of fog released around someone singing on a stage. It seemed clear that the smoke from a stove could kill a person, but the smoke surrounding a pretty woman might not kill them. Maybe it was just that she wanted to say something in her sad song and didn't express it very well, so I felt as though her breath were being choked by the smoke.

The fog gradually turned to gray. It slowly became bluish and then slowly, finally, became an impenetrable black—as if it were turning into the unimaginably opaque blackness of filthy water in a stagnant swamp. The bottomlessness of this void created a threat, like sexual desire in a woman's eyes or the infinity of a womb.

When the smiling-faced man saw my Letter of Guarantee about not needing a room from the office, a smile appeared on his face like I had never seen before. Since he always had a smile on his face, and, on top of this, he expressed everything with a smile, I could only guess at what he was expressing through this strangely different smile. The smile at this moment seemed to convey a viciousness and particular cruelty. This was the smile he had before he injected others with poison. With the poison that came along with the strengthening of this smile, he could make people squirm. It wasn't hard to understand that he was trying to infect others and himself with viciousness and cruelty. It would be easier to understand the way he dehumanized others if he had a snarl on his face instead of this constant smile.

He had already found some mistakes in that guarantee. According to him, I had changed the word *bao* (保) in "to guarantee" into the *bao* that means "to hug" (抱). The word "stay" or *zhu* (住) in a "room to stay," I had changed to the *zhu* (注) that means "to inject." As he discussed these mistakes with me, he sported a smile of revulsion as if I had written some dirty words. For a second, I thought perhaps he felt that there really were dirty meanings associated with those words. But then I realized they weren't very dirty words. If they had been, it would have been better.

You could spend your whole life learning the full meaning of these words. It's not so easy since this isn't my mother tongue—especially the second word. I use this word based on my encounters with it in books. I might have seen it in a passage describing the catastrophe of the Great Flood or in a book about sexual concepts. It is hard to get rid of a first impression, regardless of whether it is true or not. This word isn't my own word, I could only really understand it by searching for its meaning in a dictionary. This meaning was defined by others, so no matter how hard I tried, I couldn't use that word very fluently. I could get confused by the vagueness of these definitions forever. In my mind, that word has a meaning of "spurt"—like when sperm is ejaculated. But I couldn't find this definition by searching the dictionary. I don't know why I learned to think of it in this way—why I related it to spurting sperm. After I searched the official dictionaries, I found several different definitions. First: pour, like pouring liquor in a bottle. Second: flow into, for example, the water flowed into the fields. Third: drop, for example, the rain drops from the sky. All these definitions were related to water, and that may have caused my misconception.

The boss forced me to rewrite the Letter of Guarantee stating that I wouldn't demand a room. I wrote it over and over, but every time there were some mistakes. So, he would make me write it again. I was angry at myself for proving what he had said about me not being able to write a letter properly. So I insisted that I be allowed to write the Letter of Guarantee using our own language. But this made the situation deteriorate even more, because I couldn't even write it properly in Uyghur. Gradually I became unable to open my mouth in front of him. Every time I would write it slowly with so much care, and then immediately check my work. As if I were cursed, each time there was a mistake that I hadn't accounted for. When the letter was placed in front of my smug coworker, who was the boss's assistant, he would always find it. As soon as he found one, he would immediately flash the letter in front of the boss's shining face. I couldn't figure out why I always missed those damn words. They returned my sixth version of the Letter of Guarantee because of some words that were out of place. They acted as though I had intentionally written the wrong words in order to later be able to get out of my guarantee.

Ever since I was little I had a habit of seeing miswritten words as some sort of sign. I thought that miswriting these words wasn't just my own mistake, but that some sort of superpower was controlling my hand as I wrote—changing the spelling. When I wrote the word for "should live" (*yashisun*) it changed into "should vanish" (*yoqalsun*) in my homework notebook. When my father saw it, he stood there transfixed by the word. Suddenly he slapped me across the face. Immediately blood shot out of my nose and mouth like a geyser. Later, the word that came before "should vanish," unabashedly became my father's name in my memories. It was useless to blame myself for any feeling of guilt. In the end, I came to believe that I might truly have written my father's name that way. This was especially so when my father was in the last stage of his illness, and he was groaning in pain. He looked me in the eyes as if piercing them with needles, and then I really believed my memories. I wanted to avert my gaze from his enlarged eyes, so I immediately left to dump out his shit.

I looked over the mistakes they had found in the Letter of Guarantee. They were just a bunch of Uyghur words. They didn't have any bearing on whether I would rescind my guarantee not to demand a place. Even if the missing letters made the words meaningless, they wouldn't have helped me deny the meaning of the letter itself. I didn't understand why they ordered me to write it over and over. I looked at these Letters of Guarantee for a long time. There were no major mistakes that justified the way they acted. Each time I wrote it, there was just one word mis-written. There were no other mistakes that were more apparent than this, but this was enough of a reason for them to give me a ridiculing look and laugh at me in a forced cackle, while saying there was no such word as this in Uyghur. In truth, this was a mistake I really shouldn't have made. I arranged those Letters of Guarantee that I had written seven of sequentially in front of me. I looked at them and realized that I really didn't know why I had thought of arranging them like this. I started combining the letters I had missed in each of them. Just then I started, and a sudden chill came over me like I was naked in a blizzard, because the word that came from adding all the letters together was my father's name, exactly.

As I walked the length of this cold and dark street, suddenly a smell touched my senses and made me feel a bit of warmth coming from somewhere else. I gradually came to realize what this simple and familiar smell was. It was a typical smell in the city, the smell that comes from the encounter between water and human bodies in a public shower. In that shower room, everyone was naked, but nobody felt lust.

I was thinking about how to build a relationship with the city I was standing in. The paper I saw in front of the office and the numbers on it seemed to be giving me a way to do so. I believed that whoever knew the secret codes of the universe would know his fate beforehand, because he himself would be inside those secret codes. Because he would already know that his body and soul were constituent parts of the universe, he would be united with it.

Just then it seemed like everything was vibrating and changing in the fog. There was an infinite number of things to count. I succeeded in stopping myself from counting the windows that shone dimly in the fog, since I already had so many numbers from that paper. I felt as though those numbers were enough for me. For the first time my greed for numbers seemed satiated.

When I was young, I used to play with letters in my *Alphabet Reader*, changing them into numbers. Then I would feel as though I were a hero who had done some kind of secret and dangerous thing. This made me really happy. But I knew anyone could figure it out because it was so simple. I really wanted to express some secret, esoteric thing that no one could understand with numbers. But no matter how hard I tried, I felt as though I couldn't follow all the secrets that numbers could express in the outside world.

In the office I opened the drawer in front of me until it touched my stomach and periodically looked down at the numbers on that paper. I didn't eat anything, even though my stomach was really hungry, since if I did I would get sleepy, and my head would become clouded. I had to stay wide awake until I could figure out this problem. I felt as though my imagination didn't come from my brain, but from the gnawing gaps in my stomach. If I ate something, those spaces would get filled, and the insatiable desire in my brain would halt.

If I were to assume that the ten at the beginning of a number might be the month in a date, I wouldn't be able to make sense of a number such as forty-six if it were to appear next. I don't know why, but I wanted to insist on thinking of ten as the month. It was too difficult to explain since the number forty-six followed after it, and there was no month with forty-six days. After I thought for a while, I forced myself to accept the idea of the forty-sixth day of October. This number pressed down on my head like the sour smell of cigarette smoke. Where can you find a forty-sixth day of October so you can say that this day exists! I had mocked myself for considering the possibility of it as a date. But the paper was shaking in my hands as though they were in the hands of someone with Parkinson's. The numbers were swarming in front of me. Then I thought that perhaps it might be a telephone number. I added one digit to the end of it and started dialing that number. My fingers stopped trembling after I stuck them into the numbered holes on the telephone dial.

Just then, I thought I saw something scattered on the road. The objects seemed a little bit white at first, but as I got closer they seemed yellowish and then finally reddish. I discovered that they were apples. They made everything on the road look like it had also been scattered. The people walking on the road, the buildings to the side, the trees . . . everything was scattered.

An important part of the city was the myths about the endless murders and unreasonable violence that happen here. They made the city mysterious and sophisticated. I gradually came to understand that screaming fits could suddenly rise up in the street. Physical violence could happen anywhere. While I wandered about without finding even a place the size of a tomb in which I could fit my body, at the same time others lived in apartments in giant buildings, cruised the streets in fast cars, and ate piles of food in restaurants; I began to hate people. Even though I was the shyest person in the world, I wanted to destroy those fancy buildings. Would they let me to do this? In others, this kind of hatred sometimes turned into action. Occasionally pushing some to carry out murders and acts of violence, their depression mixed with fanaticism. Stabbing people randomly in the street came from their resentment toward the city. The thing they were stabbing wasn't a particular person, they were stabbing the city's rejection of their love. For others, this resentment was only a matter of overwhelming fear. They began to fear everything in the city, even after they had already become part of it themselves.

I kept searching and searching, looking at the numbers on the front doors. A cat suddenly appeared behind me on a small ledge, took a glance at me, meowed, and disappeared. I stood there hoping that it would come back, and then I continued walking. Under the place where the cat had disappeared was a very odd window. It was unclear if it was the window of a warehouse, shower, or toilet. Based on its small size, I thought it couldn't be a place where a person would live. Since the windowpanes were really dirty, I couldn't tell what was inside, but still, there were curtains hanging in the window. People don't usually hang curtains in a toilet, so it didn't seem to be a toilet. On top of this, I noticed that there were iron bars on the window. But since city people often use bars even when there is nothing to steal, I couldn't be sure what this signified. While I was thinking about this, I noticed something hanging from the iron bars. I looked closely and realized that it was a condom. The scandalous way this condom was hanging seemed really laughable to me. People cover their bodies with veils so seriously, but even the most secretive things, things that were filled with their bodily fluids, they could exhibit openly by hanging them from a window.

There was the smell of a burning chemical substance from somewhere, of trash being burned. The smell of burning garbage always gave me different feelings. Sometimes, if the smell was strong, it made me want to vomit. Sometimes I wanted to smell the scent of it for a long time. The smell that came to me now seemed to be that of a woman's longing. When I was younger I had developed a sinus disorder, so my sense of smell was oversensitive. But I didn't feel depressed by this. These smells have become the only thing that can bring sense to my life. Whether we notice them or not, these smells exist around us. Our lack of ability to sense them is a way of wasting them. The oversensitivity of my nose gave me the courage to live. Because I could detect scents that others couldn't, my experience with them was deeper than that of others. This meant that I was both living together with others, and at the same time living more fully.

I noticed that this smell seemed to be coming from a pile of trash in a building that had been flattened after being torn down. A child stood at the side of the road holding a reed broom that was taller than he was. He seemed to be too small. His dark, skinny body seemed hunchbacked. He looked down in fixed way. Taken together this scene resembled a grave marker made of bricks leaning against each other in a cemetery. He stood there, not moving his eyes. The rats were making a sound in the trash that resembled the sound of rain on dry leaves, or the sound a storm makes when it blows through the ceiling and makes a kid's body shiver. He stood there stock-still in front of the trash. It was hard to guess why he was standing there like that. He might have been hoping to find a bottle of something that he could drink to make him have crazy thoughts. Or perhaps he was hoping to find someone else's discarded toys here and there.

At a water pump, a woman was pushing strongly on the handle to pump water into her bucket. Her eyes were focused on the water that was streaming into the bucket. As she saw me getting closer, she quickly stopped pumping water, lifted the bucket, and walked away. The area around the pump was very slippery because of the way water was continuously flowing, so as she walked away she almost fell down, several times in quick succession. Each time the water in her bucket splashed out a little bit onto the ground. The water that stayed in her bucket seemed to become less and less. She walked very quickly, entered a narrow alleyway, and disappeared. Her pace frightened me a little; it seemed to signal that she might bring out some other people who would grab me by my collar and accuse me, a Uyghur man, of raping her. After I saw this, I wanted to run, but I needed to find a room in which to lay down. It would be horrible to stay in the street, so I pushed aside my fear and forced myself to keep searching.

I heard a rustling sound and stopped and looked to the side. I couldn't see anyone there. The fog floating around the rubble and trash heaps gave this place a threatening character. The endless rustling sound that came from this rubble caused my body to shiver instinctively. I carefully noticed which side the sound was coming from and confirmed that it came from a pile of trash. In this garbage, many living beings were scurrying around. They were just like the people in the streets of the city: moving very quickly, bustling this way and that. The whole content of their lives, which was comprised of eating, sleeping, and procreating, seemed to resemble the lives of the people of the city as well. Those creatures, which we don't even want to imagine, and which make us nauseous, were secretly enjoying eating, sleeping, and procreating—making a holy crime of living.

I saw a corner of a wall that looked like it had been decorated as someone's living room in the middle of the ruins. It was glimmering in a disagreeable way that revealed the fakeness with which they had given beauty to the house.

The ashes piled in the room formed a heavy mound in the brick rubble. There were embers still glowing in the smoldering ashes like an infected wound. There were also several pairs of socks and one pair of pants in the trash. I couldn't get over the feeling that someone might want to wear them and that hungry viruses, which had become starved after the clothes were abandoned, were waiting impatiently inside for them. Those viruses would infiltrate someone's body via the tiniest of capillaries and then rapidly multiply, taking over the person's life like a plague.

I don't know anyone in this strange city, so it's impossible for me to be friends or enemies with anyone.

I was choking like an infant in the process of being born, thrashing to escape the amniotic fluid of the womb. This road was like a birth canal—narrow and infinite, cloudy and churning. Like the fluid that creates life, everything was lightly glowing, like light reflecting on the moist ground in the darkness where life begins. The vague glowing of the moisture on the ground made me understand why people had so much hatred toward sex and life.

The smiling face of the smiling-faced creature who sits facing me was energetic, hopeful, vigorous, full of mental strength, as if he controlled the whole world. He seemed so powerful and worry-free . . . sometimes he even hummed a song. But the brighter his smile shone on his shining face—which glowed annoyingly as if it were polished—the more the expressions behind it were revealed: hopelessness, sadness, and listless depression. The more these affects were revealed, the happier and more energetic he would appear. But he couldn't hide anything from me. It was as if his inner organs were secretly bleeding and gradually he was becoming bloodless. His shining face was actually an indication of the process of losing the light that comes from the power of living as it was being replaced by a creepy, dark, and fetid light—a sign of death. Under his shining skin, there was a disease festering. It was just that the plague were running rampant, masking a clear view of it.

But I avoided letting him know my dislike for his annoying face, because as soon as I walked outside, I erased it from my mind's eye. His face would blend into the endless sea of faces in the street. His face became as strange to me as the faces of any of the other strangers floating down the street. I didn't have any connection to him. He just coexisted with me in the same way that chairs, shelves, a typewriter, or a mop in a corner existed.

Somewhere a door opened with a loud creak. A child around the age of seven or eight ran out breathlessly, unable to cry due to his anxiety. Then the sound of cursing could be heard through the dirty wood of the door and an enraged man ran after him in his underwear. The appearance of this man was unimaginably weird. His eyes were red as if they were filled with blood. The kid ran a little farther, and then stood and looked at the man who was running after him, trembling with fear. He was looking for safety and trying to find a way to escape. His eyes darted this way and that. The kid's father was telling him that if he came back he would kill him, cursing him into nonexistence. Every time he cursed the kid, he described in minute detail each action he would take as he killed him. These words seemed to pierce the kid's heart as if he were experiencing each of these murderous procedures one by one. He couldn't move closer to others due to his shyness with strangers. He stood to the side staring in a green-eyed squint at a fixed point for a long period of time. Although his face was copper colored, due to its bloodlessness it appeared a bit white, and the liver-colored hair loosely covering his face made him appear small and thin. The fear in that kid's eyes and narrow forehead seemed so familiar to me. I recognized him immediately. I saw in his eyes my own character that I had inherited from my mother and physical traits of my father. Because he was staring with extreme confusion, hopelessness, and fear, his eyes were greatly enlarged. It was me. The man who was running after him was my father.

Everything is temporary. Everything is variable. This was the thing that saved that kid from suffering. But this plasticity, this instability, is also the thing that makes humans suffer in hopelessness. They worry about the way things are changing in front of their eyes. They want to have unchanging values, standards, and constitutions. Stable homes, stable incomes, and stable jobs. But those things are always changing. Childhood becomes adolescence and adolescence becomes old age. Summer changes into winter and winter changes into spring. Things change ceaselessly. People don't know what to do when things suddenly disappear in unpredictable ways and are replaced by other things. If that happens, they just lose their minds. People always dream of having things that never change. This is not due to a fear of aging or because of missing the past; it comes from a fear of uncertainty. Perhaps this is one reason that people hate the city. The city changes too quickly; sometimes you can't find a huge building that you just saw yesterday, no matter where you look. You can't know what the world will become tomorrow. People in the city have a tremendous amount of difficulty imagining tomorrow, because buildings surround them on all sides, and they don't have the space to imagine. But I, on the contrary, enjoy the variability that makes so many other people anxious and uneasy. It gives me solace because it indicates that everything will disappear.

The fog hit my body like anesthetic hitting someone lying prone on an operating table, gradually making me powerless, numbing my senses. The farther I walked into the center of the fog, the further it seeped into the center of my mind. The dimmed senses of my body mixed with the fog and turned my mind into a cold, inert, lifeless, unchanging, and seemingly undeniably virtual state.

I could sense in the fog that smell that forever lingers in a house where the smoke from cigarettes has leached into the walls and the household items. Even if you open the windows, it won't dissipate. The heavy choking sound of the fog, which was like the breathless moaning of a dying patient, seeped into the nooks and crannies of my bones. My knees trembled powerlessly. My body was gradually starting to float, spreading out into the fog. I didn't know why I couldn't get rid of this unreasonable feeling. I imagined a cigarette in one trembling hand being inserted into a dry, cracked-lip mouth. The skin of this hand was crinkled with dryness and covered with small black spots. I didn't smoke because I had seen the last tremble of that hand and because of my fear of death. After he inhaled from the cigarette several times, his face became even paler and the skin on his face constricted in a trembling way. In spite of this, his eyes and cheeks expressed a sort of satisfaction and he seemed to be like someone who had come back to consciousness after undergoing a serious issue. My whole life had been filled with the sour smoke of cigarettes. Because of this, as I grew up, my face, naturally a coppery red, had become dark and sallow, lifeless as the dried bark of a tree. I thought that perhaps this was because I myself had been smoked by the sour smoke of the hand-rolled cigarettes.

It surprised me to see that there was a tree in the street. I didn't remember seeing a tree the first time I had passed by this way. It was difficult to imagine the existence of the tree in the street, and because of this it seemed melancholic, like a forgotten dream. There were only a few branches left. Its bark was painted white, making it appear fake. A thin rope hung from one of the branches and swung in space. I imagined someone being hung from it. After I looked more closely, I discovered that it actually wasn't a rope but a twisted electric wire.

In the scrubland far from the village, flocks of sheep were grazing. The children were lying beside the streams and springs full of water, watching their sheep. They swam in the springs. They played naked, running here and there. They gathered and watched the screaming male donkeys running around the scrub-lands mounting the females with a kind of bottomless desire. This primitive and explicit action excited them. Although it was clear to me what they wanted to see, perhaps since I myself didn't want to really understand, or couldn't really understand, even now, I never really understood what was happening.

There was a swampy smell that came from the scrubland. It wafted again and again behind your nose. It seemed to seep into your body and make you part of the scrubland. It seemed as though bitter grass might grow out of your body. I had let the sheep graze and laid there in the scrubland side by side with my neighbor's dark-skinned daughter for a long time. I had been waiting see how the grass would slowly sprout from my body.

I wanted to measure her height using my hand span. But she rejected this idea, saying that measuring someone's height would make them shrink. I wanted to measure the parts of her body: the rise of her breasts, her hips, and the length of her legs. I wanted to calculate the numbers that resulted from these measurements in different ways—their roots, multiplies to the second power, differentials, integers—and analyze what these numbers might mean.

I used to really like going to school. Although I was often bored with the classes, school made me really happy. At school I could avoid my father kicking and insulting me. In class I would look at our neighbor's dusky daughter from my desk two rows behind her. I would eye her and assess her dimensions. Her neck, shoulders, the circular slope of her back, and the other geometrical shapes of her form attracted my attention. At noon we used to sit and dip our legs in a stream of muddy water. She would lightly press her heels into the water until the toes of her dark feet began to blend in the water and could not be clearly distinguished from the upper parts of her calves. Once she had laughed and showed me the way the underside of her foot had become lighter in the mud. She said that if someone were to drown in the water, that person's skin might turn that color as well. I told her that if I died, I might turn green like corn bread that had been stuck in an eddy for too long.

The beauty of a person is actually the beauty of their dimensions: from their height to the width of their waist and chest. The symmetry between a person's right and left sides. The right side is like the shadow of the left side, or the left was like the shadow of the right. If this symmetry breaks, it will ruin the aesthetic appeal of their beauty and their sense of balance. This might have been the source of my fear of falling too often, which I had from childhood. The sense of wholeness that comes from the symmetry of a person's left and right sides was actually just an inversion of this.

I was still eyeing and calculating the different dimensions of her body. The symmetry of the dimensions of her body seemed deeply broken. I noticed that one of her shoulders was higher than the other, and one eyebrow was not level with the other. Her lips also sloped a little to the side. These features gave a person a feeling of being tilted. It was clear that this tilting was related to a propensity for falling. When I was a baby, I struggled with using my feet. When kids my age were running wild playing with each other, apparently, I was just plopped down in the rubble of a ruined wall, flashing my bluish butt through the split in my pants. So, my experience with the fear of falling was deeper than everyone else's. The reason I wouldn't drink alcohol was also because of this. I figured that when a person got drunk, his head would become dizzy, and his body would lose its balance.

There was a twisted-legged man who came out of the fog. I stopped in my tracks and looked at him because I thought he resembled someone who had vanished from my memory. The person I remembered's middle teeth had been falling out. In order to hide this deficiency, he wouldn't laugh openly. He even worried that others would notice that he was deliberately hiding his laugh. So when he laughed, he laughed out of the side of his mouth without opening it. Because this wasn't his normal facial expression, it seemed fake. What I remembered about him was just small fragments that couldn't explain why I had thought of him. In the environment where I grew up, he was analogous to a random thing stuffed into a crack by a plasterer who couldn't get ahold of enough mud to build an adobe wall and, in his anger, continued making walls with whatever he could get his hands on. Or he was like a desert date tree at the corner of the road. Or he was like the unevenness of the hand-formed walls in the place where a person would go to pee with his head sticking out in the open air. That person existed just like all of these things. It was a sort of existence that was very familiar, yet completely unrelated to me. This man was the husband of my unspeaking sister. A strong smell of manure hovered about him. For a few days prior to today, I had thought about how he had resurfaced in my memory. This might have been because he had left a deep impression on me, but I had later forgotten. By thinking for a while, at last I remembered his deep voice and his whining cry. The way he cried was so ugly that anyone would find it tedious, and it would fill them with misery. Everyone was bored by the sound of his crying. They all complained about it, saying it was even less pleasant than a person walking in a wobbly way on the edges between the fields in the village. But he wouldn't stop crying. Crying, especially crying in order to bore other people, was his only means of survival. This crying sound was like the sound of a swarm of buzzing bees; I couldn't get it out of my ears for several days.

When the person got closer, I no longer felt that he resembled the person in my memory. He walked dangerously close to me. Perhaps he couldn't see me clearly in the fog, so that is why he walked so close. I wanted to ask him about what I was looking for, but I got stuck after I spit out the number of the residential area, because my voice was constricted by the thickness of the fog. The sound seemed to move slowly toward him, as though it were floating suspended in the fog and couldn't reach his ears. He passed me as if he didn't see me, and I was surprised at myself for thinking that he resembled someone I knew.

I looked back at his vague silhouette in the fog and listened for that crying sound, but he was vanishing very silently. He left an icy cold space in the spot where he disappeared. I looked at that spot for a while without moving my eyes. Then I remembered the man he reminded me of. I thought he cried because my language-deficient sister had left him. For a long time, I had thought that this was the case. Actually, he was crying because he had lost the work brigade's cow. But his crying hadn't impressed others in the way our model workers had when they put their clothes on the work brigade's sheep in order to protect them from cold—even though they had almost frozen to death themselves. To others, being abandoned by a woman was equal to revealing a physical deficiency that shouldn't be revealed. Maybe I thought he was crying because of this, like a person who screams when he comes to consciousness after his leg has been amputated. His hand-me-downs appeared frequently for me, but he himself came seldomly. After my sister disappeared and I got up to put on my clothes, I found that my own clothes had vanished. I looked everywhere, in the sheets, under the rugs, but those clothes were nowhere to be found. Due to this, I couldn't go out for a day because I didn't have any clothes. Later, I discovered that my sister's husband had taken away my clothes since they were an altered version of his clothes. Of course, I wasn't the collective's sheep, so no one was willing to take off their clothes and give them to me to cover my naked body.

The worry, confusion, loss of consciousness, and dreaminess that happened in the city was related to people's bodily experience. When people were surrounded by skyscrapers, luxurious lights, and an environment full of smoke, their bodies were transformed in mysterious ways. They began to gather weird smells, especially if they were not constantly cleaned, and they began to produce disgusting waste, even though they were also eating luxurious food. Their bodies became mysterious, dreamy, and virtual things. This confused their vision, made them worry, and turned their dreams into fantasies. People hoped to escape into those imaginary scenarios and disappear. Fearing the city is in fact an expression of fearing the self. When people begin to think of their bodies as part of the city, then the depression and poverty that comes from the city makes them groan hopelessly.

I felt like the fog wasn't in a gaseous state but rather in liquid form. It was splashing over my body like the sea. I couldn't make sense out of hearing its silent voice. I don't know why, but I was worried that others would know that I felt this way. Perhaps this was because they didn't have this sort of feeling and people don't want others to possess something that they don't share in common. They might become angry if I have a feeling that I don't share with them, and because of this they might kill me. So I thought I shouldn't reveal to others what I was fantasizing. But they will use every conceivable method to know someone else's thoughts. For them, fantasizing secretly is a crime.

One day a woman appeared in my office building. Maybe she had been there before. Maybe I just didn't notice her earlier. So maybe it just felt as though she was a new arrival in the office. Her skin always had a tallowy glow as though polished with cooking oil. This seemed very funny to me. When I saw her arms emerge from her short-sleeved shirt, I imagined what it might be like if I were to grab it. This didn't emerge from a sexual desire, but because I was curious about why her skin shone so much. It seemed that even if I were to grab it, it would just slip away because it was so smooth. It was hard to imagine what this kind of smoothness might feel like. I thought about feeling this slippery smoothness one time when I was beside her. I suddenly wanted to grab her arm, but I controlled myself with much difficulty.

I saw her in that condition for only a few days, because later the weather turned colder, and her clothing gradually became heavier and heavier, and her skin took on a new mystery. After this, every time I saw her, I couldn't believe that she was the same person whose skin always used to have a yellowish glow as though polished with cooking oil. When she spoke, she plainly had a congenital defect on her face, the kind that crops up when there's too much intermarriage in a family. This made her easier to forget.

Gradually the impression she left on me began to disappear, and my image of her took on another form.

Except for the glow of her body, there was nothing else about her that was attractive. If she were to show her naked body to a child who had never been close to a woman before, perhaps that child would look at her with surprise. But if she were to stand naked in front of me, I might not even notice her. Although she did walk around almost naked in the summer, her thick tallowy skin prevented me from thinking that she was, in fact, almost naked. On the contrary, when she wore thick clothes in the winter, a little bit of beauty did emerge from her body—leading a person to notice her. Perhaps this was the reason I hadn't noticed her before. But I had intimate feelings for all women—as if women were born in this world in order to give the world love. For me, the idea of a woman insulting others with ugly words is an unimaginable thing. But the face of this woman seemed to become more and more swollen day by day with anger. Whether this was because the anger inside her was migrating toward the outside or due to a reaction to the cosmetics she was using, the skin of her face seemed to be turning bluish. The first thing she said to me was hateful. I stood there, surprised, as she said she would drink my blood. I didn't know why she said this to me, a Uyghur man. I still don't know now, either. Perhaps I will never know. And I'm not that interested in knowing the answer. What value is there in knowing it anyway? But later, when I realized that I needed a room, then I felt her insults were more like threats. Yet at the same time, it seemed impossible to know why she did this to me. I asked some of the others, but no one could give me an answer. They could only make various absurd, hilarious assumptions, though they wouldn't have felt that way to her. Others asked me whether I might have said something bad about her behind her back. I couldn't even recognize her, so how could I have said something bad? I told them even if my boss had ordered me to say something bad about her, I wouldn't have been able to. Finally, I just gave up on figuring out why she had insulted and threatened me and accepted her existence as a reality, just as I might have accepted the existence of a wall. But she said she wouldn't allow me to stay in the office any longer. Because she knew that I had no place to stay, she always spied on me, suspecting that I would spend the night in some dark, barely noticeable corner. I would feel her presence like rat poison. Because of this, I didn't dare spend the night in a corner of the office, even though I couldn't find any place to go.

When they were collecting money at the office for victims of a disastrous flood, I refused to donate anything. Everyone began to murmur among themselves. It was on that day that I first saw a change in the faces of two of my dead-faced colleagues. They were surprised and shocked, as if they had encountered something unimaginable. This expression stayed on their faces for a while and then they slowly returned to their original state. Initially I thought that perhaps this expression would be fixed on their faces forever. Perhaps it would even become the final expression of their faces. But after a while they slowly returned to their original state.

The woman whose skin had a tallowy glow as though polished moved her mouth, which smelled sourly of onion and garlic, close to me as though she wanted to kiss me. In an unbalanced mental state, she hissed that people across the whole world, even our enemies, were mourning this disaster. She asked me why I was so uncaring. She said that I had gone beyond the limit of propriety. It wasn't that I couldn't bear the words she said, but that I couldn't stand the smell from her mouth. So in the end, I gave a donation. It seemed as though, if I hadn't done so, she would have continued to speak in my ear until the end of the meeting.

Apart from the money that I had donated, the money I had to give to the people who donate blood, and the money for the government bond that the office gave to the janitors, I was left with less than half of my salary. That amount of money could be spent on just a few meals. After I donated the money, I counted the money out loud, and told everyone else to count their money by hand in order to let them know the difficulty with which I would pass the next month. But it seemed as though no one else was interested in knowing how much money was left in my hands. I told them that my condition was even worse than those whose houses had been destroyed in the floods, because I didn't even have a house to be destroyed in a catastrophe. After they heard this, they were even more angered at my inhumanity. This was because for them, the important problem was not my living condition but the way I had refused to admit to their moral superiority. Every word I used to justify my position made me guiltier.

The infinite darkness in the skies of the city was crashing on the shores like the infinite waves of the sea. Every time they rebounded from the shores, they would join the lustful cries of women and heavy breath of men from dark windows, just as the waves returned the trash and fruit abandoned on the sandy shore to the sea.

Just at that moment an iron gate opened with the heavy, creaky sound of iron meeting iron.

I looked to the side of the open door and saw a man walking out, pushing his bicycle. There was no one seeing him off. Because of this it was not hard to guess that he was the owner of the house. I immediately walked in front of him and asked him for the right direction to that damn room. But this man, who had a face as firm as cast iron, didn't seem to fit into this big city's desire for beauty and lust. His appearance didn't correspond with any shared feeling between humans. I couldn't imagine that any chemical reactions were happening within him. It reminded me that in general people's imaginings about the big city were just completely fantasies.

In any case, his face was solid and had no expression. It was like a floating corpse or shadow in the street. Like the feeling one got when speaking with the dead, it made me, a Uyghur man, feel uncomfortable. The wrinkles on his face, which expressed both laughter and constant crying from over-exhaustion, seemed as though they could no longer move.

My question didn't achieve any change to his face. I was standing right in front of the door, blocking his way. He pushed me strongly aside with the handlebar of the bicycle and kept on walking. The metal of the bicycle dug deeply into my ribs. I staggered back a few steps and sat on the ground with a thud. He just walked away, not even casting a glance in my direction. His bicycle disappeared into the fog, but the sound that came from the bicycle jumping on the rough pavement could be heard for a long while as a kind of groaning.

An abandoned shoe on the side of the road was detached from its sole. It sat there open-mouthed, like a barely breathing man who still wanted to continue walking—the toe of it open to an endless succession of destinations. Its loose strings seemed to be waiting for its owner to come back and fasten them again. Some Uyghur boys think that if the smell of male sweat from inside a shoe after it was taken off reaches the nose of a magnificent woman, it might overwhelm her—because to them it didn't resemble the smell of a dead body, but rather the way a young man's energy couldn't be contained in his body.

I tried to imagine how many houses that shoe had entered before, how many passages it had walked through. How it had been taken off and placed under a platform, spreading the strong smell of sweat through the house, adding a new mood to the atmosphere of the house.

A little white dog ran past me and disappeared immediately in the fog. From the place where the dog had disappeared, a man shuffled toward me, hunched over as if he had a sexually transmitted disease. His appearance in the place from which the dog had just disappeared made one think that the dog had walked into the fog and been transformed into a person. When I questioned him, he stopped, shocked, and looked at me in an idiotic way. I thought he didn't understand or hear me clearly, so I asked again. But he still stood there like an idiot. I looked carefully to determine his ethnicity, and I felt that I hadn't misrecognized him as a Han man. But it was as though he was from another people and couldn't understand my words. As I thought about asking in Uyghur, he started to speak. He said he didn't recognize me. I was surprised when I heard this because I had only asked him where a room was in a particular residential area, and where that residential area was located on this street. He just needed to answer that. He didn't need to recognize me to do this. I told him that I had to find that room and asked him if he knew where that place was or not. But he still didn't answer my question and instead repeated that he didn't recognize me.

I begged him to show me the way to that room again and again. He asked me where I worked. I answered him. Then he asked for the exact address of the office where I work. I told him this too. He continued questioning me. He asked how many people worked in my office. I'm not sure why he asked me all these questions. I kept answering the questions that I was sure I knew the answer to. But he still just asked me what kind of a man I was, until I fully introduced myself. After I had answered one of his questions, I asked him again where that damn apartment was located. But he avoided answering and kept asking me questions. It seemed as though his questions would never end. Even though the fog obscured the form of his face, it didn't have any effect on his eyes, which looked at me with doubt and disbelief. I wasn't asking him for a loan, but maybe he thought that answering my question would cost him in the same way. This was no different than the boss who told me angrily while looking into my eyes to stop looking at the clock in his office whose door was always open. He thought that sticking my head into his office to look at his wall clock was a kind of acquisition without payment. Every time I looked at it I got the feeling that he thought I was taking something unseen from the hands of the clock. It also made me feel as though I was person who always wanted to get something I didn't deserve. This was why I answered every question from the person standing in complete disbelief in front of me very seriously, one by one. But still I couldn't get him to believe me. He even asked how old the boss of our office was. I told him I didn't know. How was I supposed to know the age of the head of our office? He wasn't one of my relatives. Just then I remembered that I didn't know the age of my lost brother, or even the age of my sister. The disbelief on his face suddenly turned to anger. For a second, I thought the expression on his face was bewilderment. After I told him I didn't know, he just walked away without a word. What I realized as he walked away was that when he had initially started staring at me, it wasn't out of surprise but had actually been anger all along.

At that moment, my cold body began to crawl forward slowly as though it were a whirlwind that had lost its direction. I felt as if I were the last gasp of the earth.

I realized that I missed the smell of weeds on the body of our neighbor's daughter. This smell, along with the smell of the heat of the summer, was making me painfully nostalgic. Her sweaty skin had turned dark in the sunshine, and it felt as familiar as my own body in a simple and intimate way. It wasn't mysterious and strange like the white skin of a city woman. It didn't make one feel intimidated. Even though I had never touched a woman's body directly, I could imagine what the feeling might be like if my body were to touch that body.

She slid over a little as if she wanted to sit a bit closer to me. Once I realized this, I felt my breath accelerate, even though I acted indifferent, like nothing was happening. She might have wanted to know how I was responding to her actions, so she looked into my eyes and whispered in my ear, asking whether I loved her or not. When I heard this question, I involuntarily looked into her eyes—perhaps because I wanted to take note of her mental state. The capillaries in her big eyes had already turned red. The more she looked at me the grayer her pupils seemed to become. She looked away for a second and then looked again. I was still there, staring into her eyes with surprise. The capillaries around her eyes gradually seemed to become clearer and hotter. This made me remember the smell of those candy stores and the eyes of people sitting there in the smoke. Because of this, I immediately averted my gaze. She asked me again whether I loved her or not. I told her I didn't.

On that day, I was lying naked with her in the sunlight. After she heard my words, she didn't say anything and let me act freely. Before, she had always dodged me when I had reached out to her. Perhaps if I hadn't said I didn't love her, I wouldn't have been able lie with her like that. Maybe after she heard what I said, she had taken this opportunity to catch me. If I had not seen the capillaries around her eyes becoming red, I would have told her I loved her—in the same way that a murderer loves his own guilt.

She asked me if I loved her or not again. It was funny to me that she would want to know this. In my mind, she was like a song that I liked but whose lyrics I had never paid attention to. I didn't need to understand her, I just knew that I had affection for her and took pleasure from her. I thought this was good enough.

Before, I thought her eyes resembled twinkling stars or planets. This was the first impression she gave me. Later, I realized that her eyes didn't, in fact, shine like Venus, but rather always seemed to be cloudy. That day when I was lying with her and my sexual enjoyment was reaching its climax, I thought I wouldn't look into her eyes. But when I saw her eyes in that moment, I saw that they had become cloudy with excitement. After that I lost the feeling that her eyes were as bright as Venus, and I realized that I wouldn't be able to experience this bright feeling in the future. It was then that I understood why girls close their eyes when they kiss. At that time, the mysterious feeling that supersedes wisdom and destroys people overflows with so much power that it creates a kind of haziness.

When I told her that when I added her student number to mine it read as my birthday, she mocked me for a while. When I told her that perhaps this meant we were destined to be together, she couldn't contain herself and rolled on the ground with laughter. But something in her eyes became hazier, as if something were disappearing in the darkness.

I was looking at the numbers on the paper while shielding it slightly with my body—blocking it from the light of the office, which made everything seem pale. Because it had been too trampled, or because some sort of nail had been sticking out of the sole of the shoes of the people who had trampled it, leaving a hole in it, one number on the paper couldn't be read. I decided to read it as a zero that had been left unconsciously by others, as the disgusting odor of the office grew stronger. It seemed that that disgusting odor was inspiring me, making my imagination more and more vivid. I believe a person's imagination has a tendency to be strengthened by disgusting odors, pain, and hunger.

From ancient times there was a saying often repeated about a how a mysterious power or person, hiding under the ground like a reptile, controls the world using some cryptic secret code. The equal distribution of wealth and the maintenance of discipline was very severe in order to preserve the organizational codes that had been maintained from ancient times until now. They were like wounds that had existed underground throughout all of time. Every time I went through the city, counting the entrances of every size for each street and each corner without missing a single one, I felt as though I were walking according to these codes. When I was a kid and wrote letters as numbers or numbers as letters, I enjoyed the feeling that I was a member of that secret society. I wrote every letter of my neighbor's daughter's name, assigning them a number based on their order in the *Alphabet Reader*. I would calculate those numbers using different methods and note what would result from the tabulations. I would count the trees by the road and quite easily match them to the numbers that had resulted from my calculations of her name. On the appropriate tree I would carve the letter of her name and then keep going. I would wish that others would imagine that this was a sign of some secret organization and be terrified. But for so many years, up to the point when I left the village, no one noticed the signs I had made. Maybe the organization that controls the world by using secret codes never really existed. Perhaps it is only the result of the deep human fear that arises out of the infinite nature of numbers.

At that moment when she had asked me if I loved her or not, I had been absorbed in thinking about whether or not it might be possible to measure the relative strength or weakness of this feeling using numbers.

I don't know anyone in this strange city, so it's impossible for me to be friends or enemies with anyone.

I suddenly realized that no matter how hard I tried, I couldn't figure out where my place was, where I was, or what street I was on. Not only this, but I didn't really know which city I was in. The clarity of my thoughts faded, and I lost my perception of space. What country was I in? I gradually came to realize that I didn't even know what planet I was on. I was lost in the infinite universe. Just then I realized that everyone becomes a homeless wanderer after they are born and has difficulty finding a proper place for themselves as soon as they touch the ground and let out their initial cry. They will spend their whole life trying to determine their position—becoming anxious and griping about its vagueness. Everyone is a wanderer in space. Even the notion of possession carried out by those who own land, palaces, and mansions is in fact just an assumption based on imitation. Some people aren't even satisfied by owning their own lands, palaces, and mansions, but to make it their own instead want to own whole cities, countries, and the universe itself. All of this comes from a kind of worry that is based on the feeling that a person can't determine a lasting position in the universe. The more this happens, the more a person wants to own their place in the world and deny the idea that nothing can really belong to them. Or that they themselves were born into this world for no other reason than to be a wanderer for their whole life. They want to deny all of this by madly thinking that they can own things unceasingly.

Perhaps what people think, when they think that things belong to them, is just an assumption. In fact, perhaps the original form or standard of space was not in reality at all close to what they had thought it was when they began imitating it. This idea is similar to Pascal's idea that the universe is an infinite space whose center is everywhere. And furthermore, that these centers do not have any spaces around them. If everything is the center, how could someone determine their position? This is a problem because they are standing in the center of the world, while at the same time others are also standing in the center of the world. Compared to this, people's original structuring of space into districts, cities, countries, and continents is a kind of foolish game. But at the same time, as people become caught up as characters in this scenario, they nevertheless begin to think that they are actually real characters. They think that the conditions and narrative in the structure of the game are real. The funny thing is that whether or not the players know that it is a game, or if they play the game unconsciously, all of them believe that it will be dramatic and interesting. Even players who play the characters who have been condemned to death hope that it is not a made-up thing, but rather, that it is real—even though accepting the reality of it is a horrible thing for them. When the director of the play sees this, he laughs uncontrollably.

I shared a common viewpoint with others regarding the imitation of space. After I had accepted this completely, I really

wanted to know where I stood according to this common standard. But I couldn't even know this. Since I was a human, I was
forced to console myself by accepting a concept of space made
up by other people. I had to do this so that I could satisfy my
desire to know where I belong. Yet, as if the universe had suddenly vanished, I was left standing in a time in which space for
me had not yet been created.

I saw a piece of a newspaper abandoned on the ground.
I wanted to look at the date on the front page. But the newspaper was so dirty and soiled by fluid or shit that, if I were to pick
it up, it would not only contaminate my hand but also my whole
body. So I hesitated for a bit.

I picked up the newspaper with my hands and smoothed it
out carefully. Most of it had been stepped on and covered with
dirt to the point of illegibility. I walked close to a gate and read
it under the dim light. In the middle of a footprint of a big male
shoe, the following words were printed:

> Because you abandoned your wife at home one and a half years
> ago, your wife has filed a lawsuit against you in our Bureau ask-
> ing for a divorce. Since you have no clear legal residence, we have
> been forced to relay this copy of the suit and summons to you via
> this announcement. After sixty days pass following the publish-
> ing of this announcement, we will consider this a sufficient length
> of time to reach you. Following this date, if you don't return to
> our government Bureau or a court near you within fifteen days,
> we will determine the status of your marital relationship in your
> absence.

In the newspaper there was also an advertisement for a hospital's treatment for impotence and an advertisement for a missing person and so on. The part where the date was printed was

torn away. Even the date on one of the ads was illegible due to a pitch-black stain.

I heard a voice from somewhere that sounded like someone reading an incantation. This sound came out of a place in the midst of the mists, just like the way smoke floats slowly in a long, drawn-out way out of the chimney of the home of a female shaman. I listened carefully and realized that it was not an incantation from a diseased voice, but actually a song. It was as if the fog, which was gradually becoming denser, were being created by that voice. That dirty voice seemed to be transformed into this great fog as it droned on slowly. It was hard to say what instrument was creating this song. It was even hard to understand if it was a female or male singer. This lack of clarity bothered me because I realized that the richer a woman's voice is, the more attractive it becomes, but the opposite is true as well.

The fog was still swallowing me in big gulps.

The feeling of being lost engulfed my body again. I had felt this feeling only here in this city. In the same way that I enjoyed the infinite feeling of numbers, I enjoyed the mysterious feeling it gave me. Beijing, where I had lived for five years, couldn't be seen in anything but photos from the faraway village. When I was standing in it and when I was walking in its streets where I had seldom traveled, it had still felt even further away than when I had seen pictures of it in that faraway village. But even there I didn't feel disoriented in this way. It was then that I had started to doubt the relationship between the feeling of being lost and the size of the city.

Maybe I had never thought of that city as a big city. For five years, us Uyghur boys had done morning calisthenics in the sports field in the cold, our eyes barely open. We attended classes that had had no effect on our ears, but had seeped into our bodies, making our joints loose. We had eaten food that was clearly made out of dough and vegetables, but whose connection to either of those substances was unimaginable. We slept among the smell of socks and the odor of discarded food, which wafted from the washroom through the hallway and burst into the dorm rooms. We had conversations with roommates who woke up in the middle of the night about strangers who sold dumplings made out of the meat of ten or more pretty girls—out of these dumplings, the tastiest were those made out of genitals and breasts, about how some people would rape their own daughters, or about how some other people would open weird sex service places. The origins of these tales and the ways they spread among these Uyghur boys was mythical. They had no connection to the world that surrounded them in that city. In Beijing they couldn't speak with people or understand what was being said. They also described how lustful high-heeled shoes brought color to the eyes under the dim lights of restaurants, bars, and discos. It was clear that they had made up these things just by using their imaginations.

Just then, the fog, together with the darkness, was becoming deeper. The arrival of the summer was still far away. I remembered that I had no place to spend the night. I imagined that the other side of the night was even further away than the summer on the other side of the long winter. I imagined that I had to spend the night in a place that was surrounded on all four sides by walls. But that damn room didn't seem to exist anywhere on earth. I needed to find it anyway.

The fog kept infiltrating my body and gave me a heavy, cold reverberation in my dark interior. My body was turning into mud. Water and earth were mixing together, but there was no sacred breath in me.

There was a form floating out from the darkest part of the fog. It seemed as though it was a skinny man, but as he drew closer, I realized that he was tall and powerful, a big-boned, big-nosed man. From his appearance it seemed as though he had just expended a huge amount of energy, like a reptile that has just molted, but he still seemed powerful. I walked in the same direction as him, with steps as heavy as stones. Just when I wanted to ask him where that residential area was located, I suddenly realized that I should move my steps very slowly toward him. I'm not sure what impression my action of stopping after walking two or three or maybe four steps in his direction gave, but he stopped suddenly and then quickened his steps, and then after a few steps didn't even hide that he was running away from me and ran with all of his strength. I was upset by the shamefulness of him running away and so to make him worry, I thought that I should run after him for a few steps.

Shards of broken mirror abandoned on the road shone hungrily and coldly, attracting my attention. The sharp pieces were ready to hurt anyone who stepped on them.

I looked carefully at the shards of the mirror, wanting to imagine all its past reflections. The images that came to my eye were faces of fabulous beauty that had been reflected in the mirror as their owners had applied cosmetics, tracing their mouths very carefully with lipstick, sculpting their eyebrows into distinct shapes by plucking out hairs one by one and examining their faces very carefully for wrinkles around the eyes. The mirror might have also reflected women's secret actions with other men from the head of a bed or a mirror stand behind a table. Now there was nothing reflected in this mirror, as though nothing had ever been reflected in it before. It had swallowed its past, making it vanish in infinity. After it was shattered, the reflection on each shard had been separated into different realities that could not be reassembled. It might be possible to reassemble a picture that has been torn apart since the image printed on it is fixed and unchanging, but it is impossible to reassemble a scene reflected in a mirror after it has been shattered. It is similar to the way one kind of scene can be reflected differently in several pairs of eyes. Later the same scene cannot be fully reassembled from these different reflections. If a mirror is broken into several shards, the reality of a scene is also fractured into several pieces, and its reality can never be fully reassembled.

In ancient times, many people believed that many things that couldn't be seen with your eyes could be seen in a mirror's reflection. Some people even firmly believed that a person's spirit escaping from his body could be seen by putting a mirror next to his mouth as he lay dying. Perhaps in ancient times people wanted to know whether a person had breath or not, and thus mirrors became even more mysterious in their minds. Because of this, mirrors became one of the most important weapons for ancient shamans. In their minds, the real and imaginary could both be reflected in a mirror. It could reveal everything. Uyghur shamans could find extreme things reflecting through the fantasies of others. They could even talk with those images. They could uncover the most hidden secrets in people's inner worlds.

I still felt as though I were looking for my father while walking the winding streets of this city, my eyes falling asleep, and my brain slipping in and out of consciousness. The tiny droplets of rain and the sound they made as they dropped from the eves formed a dream in my mind. It was about a long chat with some other people and the murmuring sound of flowing water in the irrigation channels. I was swimming in the water, feeling both fear and joy. After a bit, the current gradually became stronger and began to sweep over me with great force. I tried to scream at the top of my lungs, but no sound came out. I began to sink and drown in the water. At that moment, a hand appeared and started pulling me out. This hand in my dream was transformed into a real hand in reality. I saw my mother's pale face stretched into a long pale shape and immediately, I woke up. I was always surprised to realize that my mother felt a threat of abandonment when she worried that my father hadn't come home at night. In fact, it was impossible that she would be abandoned by my father.

We would search for my father along the banks of the flowing irrigation channel—which I had just been swimming in, in my dream. It had already stopped raining, but the air was filled with the smell of rain. This smell slowly seeped into my nervous system and made me fearful—giving me an overwhelming feeling of sadness.

My mother, who was afraid that my father might have passed out due to being drunk, looked carefully into the irrigation channels. In fact, the one who passed out in the irrigation channels wasn't my dad, it was me. In my dream, I fell into the irrigation channel along which my mother had been searching, but she never noticed. It was weird to me that my mother would search for my father. In fact, even if she didn't search for him, he would come back in the end. He would enter the house with one hard kick to the gate. The gate had almost fallen over after so much kicking. With that kick I would awake to reality in the morning. The smell of the liquor that came from his whole body made him seem much taller. As he stumbled over the sleeping platform, the whole house seemed to shake. I would first notice the way the ceiling was rustling from the shaking, then I would look at my mother's form.

The scent that came from my father was the same as the scent of the candy. I wanted to fall asleep in that smell, and I hoped to

see the city I imagined from it in my dreams. But that mysterious city never appeared. Perhaps my imagination wasn't powerful enough to reassemble my imaginary scenes of the city. I only
dreamed of a woman who would be considered by others to be
very immoral. This woman vainly enjoyed dressing up too much.
Maybe it was the way she was always wearing clean clothes that
caused others to make that sort of assumption about her. In
their view, how a woman dressed contained the proof of her bad
intentions. They assumed that the only reason a woman wore
clean clothes was to attract men. In the village, women didn't
worry that their husbands would touch other women's bodies,
but instead that they would grab at those clothes. As if the sexy
feelings created by those clothes were stronger than the lure of
a woman's body. For them it was better for a woman to hide her
gorgeous clothes with a naked body than to hide her body with
those clothes.

I was able to get a job only on the condition that I not require
the office to provide a room. The smiling-faced man, who was
always directly opposite my desk, read my letter certifying that I
did not require a room while holding it with the tips of his long,
thin fingers. From time to time, he ran the fingers of his other
hand through his hair, his thin fingers very lightly and carefully
rubbing his short hair.

He couldn't get over how I had miswritten my own name in
the letter. He thought that I had done so intentionally. He was
sure that I would deny that I had written the letter when the
time came. But I hadn't miswritten it with that purpose in mind.
I didn't think that one or two miswritten words would invalidate
anything. If my identity could have been changed by changing
a few words, I would have exchanged those words with other,
similar words every day without end.

I had also exchanged the Chinese word "idea" or *si* (思) with another *si* word whose meaning was "death" (死). When he showed me this mistake, I laughed without thinking, because I liked these kinds of mistakes. I never thought that I could make a mistake with so much poetic meaning—especially during this time when I had no place to stay. My laugh must have stirred the poison inside him again. I knew this from the way he appeared to be flummoxed.

I picked up the Letter of Guarantee and looked through it. He still hadn't noticed that I had mistakenly written the date for one hundred years prior. Who knows, perhaps a hundred years ago his grandfather had forced my grandfather to write the same kind of letter.

There was a weird smell in the office. Even though this smell was very vague, together with the light that was always turned on during the day, it needled my brain. I felt like it made me make mistakes when I was writing. When I was just starting to work there, I could hardly stand this smell. I thought that it was the smell of my boss, the smiling-faced man. Later though, when he brought his face closer to mine and revealed the even stranger smell of his breath, I determined that this smell didn't come from him. The bodies of my two dead-faced colleagues seemed as though they wouldn't be able to spread a smell like something living—or even like the corpse of a living thing. Maybe in some corner behind the desks or in some undetectable hole, there was a dead rat. If I were to pinch my nose shut, it would affect the smooth functioning of my breathing. I wasn't sure that I would get a lung disease from this, but I couldn't stop imagining the feeling of the greenish bile that comes to someone with lung disease. Moreover, the sensitivity of my nose had increased. I told the boss that my nose wasn't only an organ for breathing, but also a vital part of my respiratory system. He told me that when he had recruited me for the office, he had given me a physical, so it wasn't possible that I had postnasal drip. Even if I did get rhinitis, he would have the right to fire me, because I had deceived others in order to pass the physical. He also said that everyone knew about these rules. After that conversation I never again mentioned increased nose sensitivity or the smell in the office.

I was hired to work for a probationary period over the autumn. During this long period of probation, I felt myself becoming a probationary object. I began to feel that my life would end at the end of this probationary period.

Before, I used to like smiling-faced people, but after I came to this office, I saw enough of that smiling rat and began to hate smiling faces. This was because the smiles of that rat were so maddeningly cruel and hateful. Although I only revealed slightly that I didn't like this sort of expression, he kicked up angrily like water that was boiling over, telling me of his position and reputation in urban society. He accused me of having no social position and no talent. He said that I didn't even have a reputation to lose. In his view, he was a famous actor who was accomplishing great things. Talking to me was not just a waste of his own time, but was actually the crime of wasting the time of his entire ethnic nationality. Yet even at that moment, when he was exploding with anger, he didn't lose the pleasant expression on his face. At that moment I truly wanted to stab a dull knife into his body and see if the expression on his face would change or not. He asked me over and over to tell him what I was good for. He repeated this sentence again and again. I told him that I had the ability to live.

That's right, the greatest thing in the world is living. There is nothing greater than living! What outraged him the most was that I was alive. It follows, then, that my ability to live must be of great value. My very existence was his greatest source of frustration.

Despite lacking evidence to prove that I had failed, he assumed the posture of a winner and hummed a song that had recently become popular. But what came from his mouth was not a sound. Rather a foul smell gushed from his mouth and spread through the air, slowly coming to dominate the space. It seemed that if he hummed a little longer, the stench of this plague would be leached permanently into the desks, walls, chairs, and even the drawer—which was all I owned in the city. Based on this it seemed that he had not won, but on the contrary, it was revealed that he had the same effect on the environment as a disease-ridden invalid or a decaying corpse.

Just then, the darkness deepened, and the fog swallowed all color and sound. In my mind, just as the essence of all sounds consisted of numbers, the essence of all colors were also numbers. So I believed that, fundamentally, sound and color were a single substance. Describing sound using colors depends on using a mathematics that is even more mystical than religion. So, for a long time, I researched the mathematical principles of color. I needed to get rid of my dependency on numbers, but the more I pulled myself out of them, the further I sank into the mud and the less I was able to free myself.

I sat in the office reading the numbers on the footprint-filled paper. I was assessing who could have possibly written these numbers. Perhaps someone had been adding something and they had written the totals down one by one. Maybe all of them were just pure numbers. If they had written these things down in the warehouse after counting them, they would have definitely written something beside the numbers to describe what each number represented. Moreover, no one would have just discarded a record of this sort of secret accounting in some random corridor. Maybe someone wanted to test a pen they had just bought and wrote some random letters. But since they were afraid that someone would come along and get some unimagined meanings from them, instead they just wrote numbers. In many people's minds, numbers are written without rhyme or reason and therefore can't have any meaning. But I thought exactly the opposite. I always thought only numbers could truly have meaning. I recognized that the words that come out of people's mouths are the same as the sounds made by two things making contact with each other, wind in the trees, water flowing in a brook, or the sound of something moving through space. Words are not any different than any of these sounds; they are just arranged in a precise sequence.

I had often seen the son of that woman, whose tallowy body seemed to be polished with oil, drawing stuff on pieces of paper. Suddenly I realized that these numbers might be something that kid might have randomly written down.

I looked at the map of the city on the wall, examining the numbers of the streets and the map legend. Who had arranged this sequence of numbers? If it had been that kid who had written them down as he played, he must have done it randomly, because he couldn't have known my height, body weight, or age. It seemed like this sequence hadn't been arranged deliberately by anyone. It was as accidental as when someone walks alongside a building and a sign falls down, hitting him on the head, killing him. It would not have happened if the sign had fallen several centimeters to this side or that, or if the man had taken a step a bit faster or slower rather than ending up exactly in the place where the sign would fall. Nor would it have happened if the sign had fallen several seconds earlier or later, before or after the man had walked underneath it.

I had seen similar discarded papers in the corridor before, but I had never picked one up and looked at it. When I looked at what was written on those papers, I had seen that they had been left by a seven- or eight-year-old kid. I might assume that this was a paper on which someone had been practicing how to write numbers, but that really didn't seem right. Maybe one of those other pieces of paper, but this time it couldn't have been the case. These numbers had clearly been written by an adult who wrote beautifully.

A little farther away there was something dimly glimmering in the middle of the road. I could tell that it was made of metal. As I walked over, I saw that it was a key that had been abandoned on the dirty ground.

After seeing the key, I remembered the strange man who scavenged for keys his whole life. He was a Sufi *sheikh* who had slept in the tombs in a Uyghur cemetery. When he died people in my village said they found a giant bag of keys beside him. People would never have guessed why he had been scavenging for keys his whole life. At first, people who noticed that he was acting in this weird way thought perhaps he was planning a big robbery, and that he was going to use the keys as part of it. The more he scavenged, the easier they thought it would be for him to open those locks. No matter how complicated the lock was, they thought, he would have a key that could open it. But the funny thing was that he never used a single key his whole life. There was no need to lock a tomb, and in the village, the houses that he entered as a guest were always unlocked. And although he didn't use these keys for anything, neither did he sell them as scrap iron. When he died, he was buried in the tomb that was his home. According to the way people in my village talked, he stared at the keys that he had scavenged for a long time every night. He looked carefully at the shape and teeth of the keys. Sometimes he giggled as if he saw something in them. Sometimes he would sink into a fantasy. Sometimes he would hum some sort of tune. Sometimes he would wrinkle his forehead. People never found out what he could see in the faces of the keys.

Where might this key be used? The key seemed fairly big. It must have been for a gate, or at least for the main door of some house. The key wasn't decayed, and it seemed likely that it had been dropped here recently. Perhaps the person who had lost the key had looked for it for a while. If it was a woman's key, she must be waiting in front of her door, unable to get in, and her neighbor must be looking at her full-formed body through a hole in his door, imagining the two of them lying together naked.

There must be more than 2 million keys in this city since it has a population of more than 2 million. Some people have not only one or two keys but rather several rings of keys. At this moment, perhaps I was the only person who didn't have a key in the entire city. I was living in this city in the space between houses that were firmly locked without a single key or access to open doors.

I don't know anyone in this strange city, so it is impossible for me to be friends or enemies with anyone.

I kept walking past houses whose numbers would get closer to the number of the house I was looking for. But when I came to the several numbers that were almost equal to the number I was looking for, I would discover that suddenly there was a gap where there was no number or that the numbers had faded into illegibility—then the house numbers would start again in a different sequence. I would begin searching again and find some numbers that were closer to the number I was looking for, but they would just disappear a little later. I assumed that those numbers must have started with an odd number on one end of the street and started from an even number at the other end of the street. But among the numbers that followed the even number sequence, suddenly odd numbers would appear. And among those that followed the odd number sequence, suddenly even numbers would appear. I also considered the possibility that one side of the street had odd numbers and the other even, but this assumption also turned out to be incorrect. I felt that the breaking of this order was one of the most uncomfortable things in the world. It seemed that the disorder in the numbers would also create disorder in the spirits of humans. I realized that the melancholy of the people in this street might be related to this disorder. The only thing that can save people from discomfort is orderliness. In one massacre that happened sixty years ago, people were killed house by house. Sometime later there was another massacre in which people were randomly killed as targets for target practice. The number of people killed in the first massacre, where people were killed house by house, was a hundred times greater than that of people killed in the second massacre. Yet people were more outraged by the massacre in which people were killed randomly. They couldn't accept this randomness. Because the massacre took place in an orderly way, it seemed like an acceptable thing to people, and they stayed silent, bowing their heads. But they couldn't stand the random killings and rose up in the streets in revolt.

The odd numbers started in the sixties, and then the numbers disappeared again when they reached sixty-seven. After skipping several houses, the numbers started again with even numbers from fifty-two to fifty-eight. On top of this disorder, the street suddenly turned at a thirty-five degree angle.

I stood for a while at this turning point in the street, not knowing what to do. There were fewer and fewer people on the street, which made me more frenzied, because a person couldn't be walking around this street at night.

The house opposite had no number, and the number of the next house was three digits. I had never seen a three digit house number before. I couldn't tell if the number of the next house consisted of three digits or four digits. Finally, I started to count off the houses that had no number or faded numbers. I was forced to guess which house was the one I was looking for. It wasn't hard to make a guess, but it might not be correct, because the numbers on the other side of the street might also be close to the one I was looking for. Thus I had no choice but to knock on the doors of some of the houses.

Mathematicians are people who are their own mystics. They use logic as a weapon.* I don't remember who said this, but they feel like my own words.

I suddenly saw a number on a door. I walked closer to look at it and was surprised to realize that it was the same number as my birth year, month, and day. It seemed to portend something to me. Even though my assumptions about these kinds of signs were always all wrong, every time I encountered this sort of coincidence, I couldn't escape my thoughts about signs. Every time it seemed as though just this once it might be a mysterious sign about my fate, and I didn't want to let its exhortation slip through my hands. In the end, just like before, all of them turned out to be a sign of nothing. Maybe this number was nothing other than the number for that house.

I stood in hesitation in front of the door after I had already raised my hand to knock, because this was not the door for a single house, but rather the gate for a small courtyard. I looked at it through the gap in the gate and noticed that there was a row of houses inside. I opened the gate slowly and walked into

---

* The author is paraphrasing Bertrand Russell.

the courtyard. Which one was the house I was looking for? I couldn't guess. There were not only no numbers on these houses, but it was also difficult to differentiate which of them belonged to one family. I moved slowly and walked a little farther inside. I stood there a while, and finally I realized I had no choice but to take a risk. I knocked on one of the doors. There was no sound from the inside of the house for a while. The lower part of the door I was knocking on was made out of wood, and the upper part was made out of glass. Although the glass was clouded with vapor, there was no curtain behind the glass, and the interior of the house could be seen clearly.

The inside of the house was dimly lit and seemed vaguely like the lifeless eyes of the prostitutes who stood on the road. Before this I had never looked into the eyes of a strange woman. I don't know why I couldn't. Except for the eyes of our neighbor's daughter, I can't remember looking deeply into the eyes of any other person. Her eyes seemed as though they were a part of my own body. Not looking into other people's eyes became my moral code after this. But one time, as I walked, I was stopped in surprise by the sound of a woman calling—because in this totally strange city I never imagined anyone else hailing me while I walked the streets. At first, I thought it was that imaginary voice that I could usually hear in the noise. I couldn't believe that there was someone who would call out to me and talk to me while I was wandering like a vagrant the first time I came to the city. I don't know why but I turned quickly and looked into that woman's eyes when she called to me. Maybe this was because what was special about her face was the vagueness of her eyes. Or perhaps because the extreme vagueness of her eyes was strange and surprising to me. Or perhaps because among humans there are people who look at others in abnormal ways, and this shocked me. Or there might have been another reason that I will never know. I stood still when I saw her and noticed that the woman's face was full of small moles, as if something were emerging from her through her face. Her face was layered with dirt. Under the dim light, the cosmetics that were smeared on her face became more distinct. They failed to hide the moles and instead highlighted them. I also found her laugh quite strange. Suddenly, I realized that what she wanted to do with me wasn't what I had originally thought but was rather a more mysterious thing. It couldn't be considered something done between people, but rather that which is done between a thief and a victim of a theft or a mugger and a victim of a mugging. It was a kind of strange, illogical relation. I shuddered at the thought of it. Before I had thought that women gave people love and many other things that humans desire. This feeling formed a kind of state in me such that I didn't even dislike women whom I would have otherwise considered depraved. Instead I felt hatred and anger only in relation to men. Yet at that moment, it seemed as though the woman in front of me wasn't giving me something but rather taking something valuable away from me without giving me anything in return—leaving me in the poorest and most miserable condition in the world.

Perhaps if the glass on the doors had been cloudy or the interior lights had provided less illumination, I would have regretted knocking on the door of this house. But because I had forced myself to have the courage to knock on that door, I had to wait there until I heard an answer from inside. Yet I knocked several times and still there was still no response.

There seemed to be several five- or six-year-old kids playing on the raised platform inside the room. A picture of a famous beauty was hanging on the wall, an upper corner of the poster dangling, creating a very white patch of color in relation to the other parts of the wall. I pushed on the door a little bit and realized it was unlocked. I asked those children whether or not this was the house that that person had arranged for me. The children looked at me and then kept playing their game. I thought maybe some of them hadn't yet started to use language. I asked those children to call their parents, but they still remained silent. It seemed as though there was a knotted-up bundle of clothes in front of the children, and they were playing around it. Suddenly a fat woman stood up from the middle of that pile. It was then that I realized that it wasn't a big bundle, but actually the form of a woman lying there on the platform. Because the stomach of the woman was so huge, when she laid down, it folded into other parts of her body and made it seem as though she were just a giant pile or a bundle of clothes.

From the fatness of the woman, I could see why she hadn't responded after I had knocked on the door so many times. After I saw the jowly face of this woman, I said hello to her. But instead of responding to my greeting, she began to insult me and, with a speed I hadn't thought possible, jumped off the platform and, without bothering to put on shoes, she lunged at me and grabbed my collar. I was so stunned by her actions. She asked me what kind of man I was, but she didn't wait for me to answer this question. She just answered it herself. According to her, I was a thief. I was frightening her kids by coming here all the time under the pretense of searching for someone. She asked me what my intentions were in doing this. But without waiting for me to respond, she said that my intentions were to kill someone. She spoke for a while like this, asking questions, answering them herself, and cursing me. Because she had grabbed my collar very firmly, I couldn't get away, and my efforts at getting away seemed even more confirmation that I was a murderer or a thief. I understood that this was happening, so I stopped trying to get away and instead I tried to explain that today was the first time I had ever come to this street, I had never taken a step on this street before, and that I was looking for building number 6891, but she never heard my explanation. Her insults were unceasing. Now she was insulting me using words usually reserved for the insults exchanged by men. Her insults focused on sex, but since she used the words used by men, her words never seemed directly related to sex, but instead they seemed to have the connotation of shit, rot, and disgusting vermin—all things that make people feel queasy. Perhaps she used these insults because she worried that if other men heard her use the usual female insults, they would enjoy the sexual feelings that came from those words.

The woman pulled me into the house with all her strength, but I resisted by holding onto the handle of the door with one of my hands. It didn't seem like she would give up easily. She said that she had noticed me lurking around here stalking her for over a year. I told her that I came to the city just one month before. She screamed and called for one of her kids to bring over a cleaver. One of those kids, who before had seemed unable to speak, found a cleaver and brought it over as fast as lightening, placing it in the woman's hand. It seemed like the woman was planning to chop my hand that was holding onto the handle of the door and pull me into the house. Although we had been arguing for a while, no one else came out. If she had a husband, what would I do? I thought that due to her screaming some of the neighbors would show up, but nobody stuck their heads out. If they had appeared, I would have been finished.

When the woman raised the cleaver to chop me, I immediately grabbed her hand. The fat arms of the freakish woman were slippery in my palm, and I felt disgusted, as if my hand had grabbed some pork. Despite this, to protect myself I had to grab it firmly. Finally, I realized that the only thing that I could do was to try as hard as possible to escape from her. Focusing all my effort, I pushed back against her, and I escaped. The woman stood there screaming. Because I was so afraid, after I reached the street I didn't stop running for a while.

I ran until I could look back and make sure that no one was following me, and then I stopped. I looked at my collar, which the woman had grabbed with her short, stubby hands, as though her hands were still grasping it. I leaned against the wall with one hand and stood there for a moment catching my breath. There was no one to be seen behind me, and I felt exhausted. I wanted to sit there leaning against the wall, but I didn't have the courage to do it. When I looked at the spot where I had rested my palm, I realized that it was a place where an ad had been pasted. Whoever had pasted the ad must have been afraid that someone else would tear it down, so they printed the ad on very thin paper that couldn't be ripped from the wall. If someone wanted to rip it off, it would just tear at the place where it was first grabbed and form a tiny rip the size of a needle. It would take an extremely long time to tear it all off. I could see that the front of the paper had been scratched at many times, but it was clear that these scratches had had little effect—the words on the paper were still clearly legible. From the many directions of the scratches, I could tell that whoever had tried to tear it off had been very upset. They might have been scratching at it in an unthinking rage. The words on the ad were large relative to the size of the paper. All of the letters were written in black, and every single word was overemphasized. The ad was jammed full of words naming sexual diseases and describing the symptoms of sexual deficiency: syphilis, genital warts, premature ejacula-tion . . . Perhaps some kids had received too much inspiration from these words, and they had drawn various elaborate illustra-tions of various genitals based on their own sexual imaginations.

Without any real reason, I assumed that the person who had wanted to scratch it off must have had a serious sexual disease. It wasn't difficult to assume this based on the outrage they seemed to feel while scratching at it. Only a person who believed that everything bad that they felt was being expressed in the ad could have ripped at it with that much anger. After I saw this, I immediately removed my hand with a feeling of shock. It felt as if the paper on which the ad was printed was itself a very dirty thing. It not only gave me a feeling of sadness, but also a strong feeling of fear. I immediately ran toward the place where the water pump was located. I wanted to pump water from it and wash my hands over and over until I was sure they were totally clean. But in order to pump water from the pump, you have to pour a little bit of water into it first. Where could I find some water? I stood for a while beside the hand pump feeling helplessly tortured.

The misspelled words of others made me imagine strange things, so I always hoped that people would misspell what they wrote and give me the chance to imagine the mystery of what those misspellings signified. In the phrase about the cure for syphilis, the ad writer had written the word "syphilis" so that it appeared that he was touting a cure for "Iblis."* How could they cure Iblis? If they could cure Iblis, and his body recovered its health and strength, he could lead people down evil paths more easily. Maybe they considered his evilness a kind of disease to be cured, and that after he was cured, he would no longer deceive people. But God had created Iblis and let him descend to earth to deceive the children of men until the Day of the Apocalypse. But deceiving humans until the Day of the Apocalypse couldn't be what that sign was signifying. When I was a kid, I thought that rat "drugs" were drugs for curing rats who had

---

* An Arabic word for Satan

diseases. Later I discovered that they used the words "rat drugs" to describe poisons used for killing rats.

I don't know anyone in this strange city, so it's impossible for me to be friends or enemies with anyone.

The room I was looking for didn't seem to exist anywhere on earth. The air of this city wasn't gaseous, but rather like a cloud of a reddish flour that made everything float away. Even the building where my drawer was located, and that person who was going to arrange the room for me, and the house number I was looking for seemed as though they had floated away. I even felt as though my own body were floating off. My confidence regarding the existence of the room was gradually becoming weaker.

It appeared that there was no one else left in the street. After I walked for a while with the intention of leaving the street, I changed my mind and instead decided to search the street one last time. Because if I didn't find a place to spend the night, I would be left on the street.

The fog was like the tongue of a dog I had seen in a pornographic video that mimicked sex between a woman and a dog. It was lapping the city silently with a sort of cold desire.

Most of the windows that lined the road weren't only used as windows but also served as chimneys. The stovepipes of the houses reached the outside through window frames from which the panes of glass had been removed. The areas around these circular pipes were filled in using small pieces of wood, and the cracks between those were stuffed with old rags. The smoke from the stoves came directly from the pipes into the street, making the fog in the street even denser. Thus, the fog in this street was denser than anywhere else.

The broken pieces of the porcelain bowls in the road called to mind a friendly family. I imagined those bowls before they had been shattered. I thought about pouring hot food into them. Beside these pieces were also some pieces of a bottle. The glowing of the pieces of the bottle reminded me of a man who was walking in the street screaming and crying openly in front of everyone. Between these different kinds of fragments there was no relationship. There was a picture of a woman's naked body that had been abandoned and couldn't have enticed anyone. Despite this, the woman in the picture was laughing unashamedly just like before. In the grim of the city the picture had become dirty, and it no longer looked like an unclad woman but instead like a miniature naked corpse lying there in the street.

Who had I been, what was I, and who was I going to be? Suddenly I felt that no matter how hard I tried, it was impossible to remember. Not only did I not even know who I was, but I also didn't know what role I was playing now. My consciousness was gradually fading. I had already lost the very concept of my identity. Now I sensed that I couldn't become anything. I felt it possible that other people wouldn't even let me be myself. I was lost in the infinite crowds of humanity. I realized that everyone became a wanderer after they were born. After they touch the ground for the first time and utter their first cry, they have difficulty finding a proper identity for themselves. They spend their whole lives trying to determine their own identity. In the end, their identity concept is only shadows that reflected their fantasies. I realized that people felt restless due to the horrors of their nightmares. Everyone was a wanderer in the universe and that the ideas of fame, power, and respect were always just a shadow that could vanish at a moment's notice. Others, not satisfied with their social positions or with the amount of fame and respect they had garnered, tried instead to live in a state of

eternal fame. A name is given to a person by others. You get used
to it when you are very young, and then begin to think that it
really is your own name. In reality, it is just a bunch of meaningless phonemes. If newborn babies are named after great people
from history, they never actually become those people themselves. On the contrary, their bodies will carry the names of
those who lived a thousand years ago, and those names include
with them the linguistic system, numerologies, and orders of
those whose names they have received. As a thinker who lived
several thousand years ago in India said, one body's senses and
the thoughts inside it are not enough to create a self. If it were a
self, it would surely totally belong to a person. But a person cannot totally control their body or every change inside their body.
If a disease suddenly appears, you don't even know which part
of your body is diseased. So how can you call yourself a self? No
matter what people call me, I just accept that small number of
sounds that people use to represent my identity, and I just try to
know who I am based on that generally known name. But I can't
even know this. Since I am also human, I am forced to accept the
concept of identity that others manufacture for me. I am forced
to prevent myself from being confused with others. Yet, at this
moment, it seemed as though I had suddenly vanished or that
perhaps I had not yet been born.

The lack of people in the street had given me a sense of safety.
If there were no one in the street for the whole night and it were
left entirely to me, of course this would be better. But if I were
to walk around the whole night, I would be exhausted and need
to find a corner in which to nap. If I fell asleep and became sick
from the cold, what would I do? Also, I needed to find people
I could ask to help me find the place I was looking for.

As the number of people dwindled, the fog seemed to be
turning from black to gray. This shade of gray was more horrific

than the earlier darkness. Amid the gray fog, my clothes seemed to be turning a faint white.

To figure out where I was, I looked farther away and tried to locate myself by looking at the tops of high buildings. But the fog didn't allow me to see the shapes of the buildings. Only the windows in the high buildings lightly glowed like mercury in the darkness—like the eyes of a cat that had been aroused.

I couldn't ascertain my location, so I chose a direction and started walking. Now everything seemed to be the same—no matter which direction I walked. Suddenly I heard an otherworldly sound that seemed to come from a tinsmith using old, atrophied tin. Then the sound suddenly stopped. Once it stopped, I realized that I hadn't even noticed the unending crackling noise. I realized it existed when it stopped, how it had been part of the sound of the street and now how it grew fainter and fainter. That was how I knew that it had been there earlier. If it hadn't stopped, I might not have realized that it had been there at all.

The smell of rot was coming to me from every part of the street. Sometimes I sensed the smell of rotten food, sometimes I sensed the various fluids that come from the body, such as vomit, sour sweat, and discharge. Even though I covered my nose with my hand, still I couldn't get away from those smells. They seemed to come not only from the street but also from my thoughts. I really wanted to vomit . . . .

Everything in front of me started to shapeshift. Suddenly the houses on both sides of the street seemed to shrink and be transformed into nests of rats. The buildings in the distance looked like beehives made of innumerable holes filled with squirming larvae and buzzing bees. Without thinking, I started to feel a desire to destroy these things. The appearance of this feeling of

so much hatred was a result of my feelings of lack and hopelessness. I didn't want to be possessed by this terrifying feeling.

The windows were flickering like the eyes of a man who was
queasy and uncomfortable.

The bit of the wall in front of me had been whitewashed.
There were a few words written there warning people not to pee
or take a shit in this spot. There was a fine of fifty yuan for anyone who shit. There was a pile of shit from a small kid just under
those words. It was the most noticeable thing in that space. It
was blooming like a flower.

I hadn't known before that fog could make a person so uncomfortable. When I had been herding sheep on the vast scrublands,
I would see patches of bluish fog floating here and there. It made
me very happy. I wanted to run to it quickly, pass through the
middle of the fog, and see how the sheep looked from within the
fog. Nobody could disrupt this kind of happiness. When I was
alone in the wilderness, I felt very light like that fog. But that fog
gradually dissipated, like fantasies that would never come true,
as the sun heated everything in the world. My happiness disappeared in just the same way. The heart-piercing heat of the sun
gave me the sign that a new day filled with extreme exhaustion
and blame had begun.

One of the basic elements in my imagined concept of the city—
the smell of candy—couldn't be found anywhere on this street.
Before I came to the city, I couldn't imagine it without that smell.
I really didn't know why I had conflated that smell with the smell
of my father's breath when he was drunk or the smell that came
from the places where people drink alcohol. There might have
been some relationship between my thrilling desire for fog in my
childhood and my desire for the big city that appeared later.

Before I came to the big city, I thought this second desire might have been because of the similarity between the fogs in low-lying areas and the clouds in the sky—the particles in them were the same. In my mind everyone has a desire for the sky. This desire begets fantasies about flying through the air and mysterious legends. When I was going through the fog when I was a child, maybe it was the feeling of contentment that made me feel like I was flying. Yet in the big city it was hard to relate the fog to clouds or the sky, as you could with the fog that was always floating in low-lying areas. No one liked the city fog.

The elementary school I went to was situated at one end of the neighborhood among some houses with whitewashed walls. Those houses were the only whitewashed houses in the neighborhood. There was a candy store in front of the school where we played. Sometimes we went into the store just to smell the candies, but the cadre member who was responsible for the store wouldn't let us take in the smell to our satisfaction. As soon as we entered the store, he would tell us to play outside and shoo us out. Even if we couldn't buy candies there, the store nevertheless attracted us with an irresistible pull. That place seemed extremely mysterious and sacred to us. We could never travel too far away from it. Later a tall kid who sat beside me began to always smell like that candy store because of the candies in his pockets. He sold them to kids whose fathers were cadres or other kids who had money. During class he always pulled candies out of his pocket, sucked on them for a bit, and then put them back in their wrappers. As he sucked on them, the area around me would be filled with the smell of candy. When he sold the previously sucked-on candies to other kids, they would complain that he had sucked on them too much and made them thin. Because I didn't have any money, I couldn't buy any candies, so sometimes I asked him if I could suck on his candies for a bit. But even though I promised that I would only suck on them for a bit, he wouldn't give any of them to me. Because of his strong association with the smell of candy, to me he seemed very strong and respectable. Even though he didn't pass the exams, he seemed smarter than other kids. Although I didn't know why, I always sided with him when he got into fights. This wasn't so that he would let me suck his candies, but because he was always surrounded by the smell of candy, so it seemed like the truth was on his side. I don't know how he came to have those candies even though he was the child of a farmer just like me. Later, when he was kicked out of school, we found out that he had actually been stealing those candies from the store.

Those who have done wrong do so because they chose the left path. I'm not sure when I started to accept this kind of logic. In the morning, before I went to school, my mother sat under the eaves of the porch, waiting for me to strap on my huge book bag and walk down the road. She mentioned that I should use my right foot first when I passed over the threshold of the door. Since I was drawn to what she was saying, I intentionally used my left foot to pass through the doorway. Of course, this purposeful action wasn't to annoy her, but rather because I wanted to hear more of her fantastic words. She didn't say anything but stood there with her huge green eyes wide open. I had never seen that sort of reaction on her face before.

After I had passed over the threshold by using my left foot first, I slept in a silence that I had never felt before that day. Although there was no noise at midnight, I woke up suddenly. Usually I slept very deeply. If I had to get up early in the morning, I had trouble opening my eyes, but on that night there wasn't a sign of sleepiness in my body. My heart was racing for no reason. I looked around silently. There was no rustling in the house. In the heart of the darkness, there was a big form sitting silently in front of me. There seemed to be a smell of seeping wounds coming from his body. At first this smell seemed quite faint, but later it became strong. I also sensed the smell that came from the candy store and the smell of sour sweat. The way he was sitting so still seemed to intensify the smell that came from his body. A while later I heard the sound of a match being struck and lit. The flame shook and trembled and didn't reach the end of the cigarette before it was very quickly extinguished. In the light of the shaking of the flame, I saw the man's face very dimly. He appeared to be my father. A match was lit again. The flame was still shaking, and it seemed as though the figure was also trembling. This time I clearly saw my father's face. As the match was almost burned out, he lit his cigarette. He gave it one hard inhale and breathed it in for a long time. The trembling of the glowing red end of the cigarette stopped shaking along with this heavy breath.

After my father saw that I was awake, he ordered me to get up. He slowly walked toward me and lit the oil lamp that was in a nook above my bed. Using the light of the lamp he moved my platform and started digging under it. I watched his movements while sitting absolutely still. My father dug at the ground madly. I didn't understand what he was planning to do, but—as if I understood—I didn't ask. Maybe I didn't have the courage to ask him. Under the light of the oil lamp, the part of his shoulder that wasn't covered by his undershirt was shiny with sweat. The more the sweat appeared at that spot, the more the smell of wounds and pus that came from his body began to fill the house. He was panting hard. From this panting it seemed clear that his respiratory system was not that good. At that time, I assumed that his nose was spreading the smell of an infection. He was digging silently. He didn't even want to stop for a breath until he was finished digging. The silence of his movement gave me a weird feeling, but I didn't know what this feeling meant. From his unceasing labor I suppose that I should have felt that there was a terrific amount of life in his body. But at this moment I just felt death and disease from his presence. All of these were misleading feelings on my part, because even after this he lived for a fairly long time, from my perspective. For many years he lived silently, like a strange creature that emerges from the underground. Then he died of liver disease.

I couldn't stand looking at what he was doing, but it was as if I had no choice. My eyes couldn't stop looking. My brain started to become very clear, but the clearer it became the more I didn't understand anything. Finally, I shifted my gaze from my father to the walls, but under the light of the oil lamp, his shadow was transformed into horrific shapes, and this made me even more uncomfortable. Before I had thought that darkness was the most horrific thing, but now I realized that the most terrifying thing was the light of an oil lamp and the images I imagined because of the shadows it cast on the walls. Under the shadows I saw on the wall was a giant portrait of a man who had a mole on his chin.* He was drawn in completely warm colors—giving him a sort of glowing appearance. I couldn't understand why that man's head was so enlarged. I didn't want to believe that anywhere in the world there could be a man whose head was equal to the size of this wall. That day though, when my father moved closer to the oil lamp, his shadow on the wall loomed larger. At one point it grew to the same size as that picture on the wall. It was then that I came to vaguely realize that the size of the form in the picture and the size of that form in reality weren't the same. Even

---

* Here the author is referring to a portrait of Mao Zedong.

though my father's shadow fully covered that huge picture on the wall, it still didn't disappear from my vision. His eyes were drawn so that no matter how you looked at them, they always appeared to be looking at you. On that day he locked eyes with me.

The air was sticky. In the air there was nothing moving besides my breath and that of my father. There were no humans in the whole world. Only my father, I, and the picture on the wall were left. It was as if my run-away sister and brother had never existed. The world was so silent. I waited for so long for a breeze to come and blow out the oil lamp, but nothing came.

After he finished digging, he led me into the next room. In the middle of that room was a form wrapped in bed sheets. My father ordered me to lift that thing with him. In my little body I didn't have enough strength to even lift one end of it. My father lifted one end of it without much effort, but I could hardly walk while dragging it on the floor. It left a wet trail as we dragged it. Because the light from the oil lamp was so dim, I couldn't tell what color it was. The warm liquid touched my hand. The spot that it came in contact with felt like it was on fire. From that time to the present, I haven't been able to get rid of that burning feeling. Maybe this feeling will stay with me forever. At times I became a person who wanted to wash his hands without stopping. Even though my hands were clean and didn't need to be washed, I couldn't stop involuntarily washing my hands. Other people assumed that this was some kind of illness and suggested that I go to see a doctor. But I refused, because I knew the reason why I wanted to wash my hands without stopping.

We placed the wrapped form in the hole he had dug. To this day I hear the *güp-pide* sound of dropping it in in the background of my dreams. My father buried it by returning the sand he had dug up before to its place. He did this very slowly and silently in front of a kid who was still not yet eleven years old.

Then he returned the bed to its place and ordered me to go back to sleep. "You sleep." Those two syllables were the only sounds that came out of his mouth. I wanted to ask him where my mother was, but my voice wasn't very nimble. At that moment I realized that I was shaking unstoppably. Seeing me sitting stock-still, shaking, my father looked at me in a questioning way. With great difficulty I asked him where my mother was with all the voice I could muster. He walked away without saying anything. I wanted to throw myself into the bed and cry for a while, but I couldn't because my throat was so constricted. From the next room I heard the sound of my father's padding footsteps, the sound of him throwing himself onto the bed and then becoming silent. My father didn't answer me, which meant he never would. The next day my father just told me not to tell anyone what had happened during the night. If I told anyone, he would bury me in that place too, he added.

Since that time, I have had to stop and use my right foot whenever I was about to pass over not only doorways and gated entrances, but also lines and cracks on the road.

My mad desire for the city had nothing to do with the way others talked about staying in the cheapest hotels filled with the disgusting smell of feet and making deals with the prostitutes standing along the street and then absconding without giving them any money. I wanted to get away from that bed, which gave me endless nightmares, forever. I would have preferred being left on the streets of a strange city and getting mugged to remaining lying on that bed.

At that moment my body was floating in the fog, filled with fear and an intense feeling of estrangement—as though I were walking through a graveyard filled with strange people. The fog was becoming unbearably dense and heavy. It seemed to be pressing down on my powerless body. The sour, hungry feeling in my stomach gradually became fainter, then vanished into a feeling of queasiness. I slowly walked forward in the fog.

In a few places there was something yellowish sticking to the paper I found in front of the office. I couldn't tell for sure what had left those traces there. It was as if they were trying to insult the numbers. Maybe I felt this way because I felt there was something sacred about numbers. I skipped over the middle numbers and looked at the last one. I had seen the four-digit number in the last row in previous rows on the paper as well. I had guessed that the number ten signified a month, but I couldn't tell what the forty-six meant. So I had given up on thinking of it as a date because it didn't make sense. The idea of the forty-sixth day of October didn't exist, but the power of this nothingness and nonexistence was stronger than the being and existence of things. I thought for a while what the forty-sixth day of October might signify. Suddenly I was struck by the thought that it might be the fifteenth day of November. The paper in my hand trembled and shook.

The first number on the paper was the beginning of all numbers. And this number was reflected in everything, was the beginning of everything. This number allowed me to appreciate the infinite nature of all things. Because all the numbers in the world were derivations of its various shapes.

The Greek philosopher Hippasus, who was sacrificed because of numbers, discovered that the diagonal of a square whose side was one couldn't result in an ordinal number. In the same way that Hippasus discovered this, my brain also seemed to be shrinking. The familiarity of that number had shocked me. I stood there for a while looking at it. Maybe I was afraid that I had misread it. Immediately I looked around to see if anyone had seen me. This was a secret like the secret of a woman's body, it should be protected from lechers.

Somewhere in the world you can write down any number. Yet two numbers that could be written together for many centuries could suddenly become impossible to combine. Of course, this had no relationship at all to mathematics. Even the philosophers who can understand mathematics in the most mystical of ways could not explain this. I'm not sure what these two numbers were exactly. Maybe one was the number for a month and the other was the number for a day. I didn't even know why they couldn't be written together in a single space. If the numbers signified a day and a month, clearly it would be repeated once a year. Then I started thinking about all the ways that dates can be miswritten. It was due to my continuous miswriting that I couldn't put those numbers together in a single space no matter how hard I tried.

I realized that those four numbers were either a date or me. Every year I had skipped writing it by whatever means possible. If for some reason I couldn't avoid writing it, I would always miswrite it. Now I realized that it was that number.

I suddenly realized in this dark, cold street that this number was that day when I had gathered my voice and asked my father with all my might, "Where is my mother?" When my father's form had completely blocked the light of the oil lamp, and when, under his shadow, I had felt my self completely disappear. The number was the date of that day. This sudden discovery terrified me. Just then, I was searching for precisely that number.

The windows were glowing hazily like the eyes of a dog that was looking at the bone in the hand of a person eating a meal.

I don't know anyone in this strange city, so it's impossible for me to be friends or enemies with anyone.

I was walking on that winding street that was as full of abandoned things as an ancient ruin. Then I arrived in a place that had more people. It was as if they had come here for reasons unknown even to themselves. They were moving very lazily without direction or intention. It felt to me as though the fog caused them to fall into that condition. The lazy movements were inexplicably threatening. The lamp in front of the next store was hanging very low. A person's form would occasionally block the light. The light from the lamp showed their bodies in changing shapes—sometimes elongating, sometimes twisting. Only from these forms could you detect the way they were moving.

I moved toward them silently. I stood there not knowing which one to ask where building number 6891 was located. One of them passed by me, bumping me with his shoulder. I almost fell over from the impact. Then another one came straight at me. In order not to be hit again I ducked to the side immediately and used that opportunity to ask for directions as he passed by me. After he listened to my question, he stared at me. I was stunned by this. He looked right into my eyes for a bit and then looked at the others around us. The others also looked at one another. A big wart on the side of the nose of this tall man made his face look different. He asked me if I recognized him or not. His question clearly revealed hatred and animosity. From his words I sensed nothing but endless anger and cruelty, so I told him I didn't understand what he was saying. He repeated his question. I told him I wasn't trying to get to know him. I just wanted to know where a room was located. He looked to the others and then accused me of blocking a stranger's way and insulted me. I was frightened and wanted to run, but he blocked my way and demanded that I tell him who I was. Feeling like I had no other choice I answered his questions. But that rat thought I was lying. I searched my pockets to find my work ID. But I couldn't find it. That rat stared at me crazily, forcing me to answer. From his stare, I could tell he was expecting my words to be a lie. His confidence about this made him very cocky. He felt as though he were getting iron-clad proof and so he was very satisfied. His self-satisfaction strengthened the cruel expression of rage on his face. Just then, his eyes appeared very familiar to me, but I knew with certainty that I had never seen him before in my life. Where exactly had I seen these eyes before? When I was a kid? When I had gone to college in that strange city, Beijing? This wasn't the only moment when those eyes had stared ruthlessly at me. I felt as though I had always seen those eyes. They appeared in my heart from the very first time I opened my eyes to the world, like a poisonous snake. They continually stung my heart cruelly, making me writhe with pain. Was there no way to escape from them other than in death?! Kneeling, crying, even dying, everything was useless under their gaze. Because a violent light emitted from those eyes covering the whole world, my tiny, completely different, lonely, skinny, miserable body couldn't be tolerated anywhere in this wide universe. The light from those eyes could infect the trash in the gutter like a plague, making it as mean as they were. As a result, the trash would become as heavy as the whole of life and the earth itself. This tiny form of mine would welcome that trash to rush down like a flood from the mountains. It would be massive, able to destroy me immediately under its crushing weight. The mean smell from this garbage would make me forget any sort of smell that might come from a woman's body.

At that moment I fell over backward from a sudden kick. For an instant I thought to stand up and run away, but then they came over and kicked me, not giving me any chance to stand.

They stomped on me for a while, but then I felt one sudden blow to my stomach that made my intestines feel sour as if something had punctured me. This pain didn't seem to be the same as the pain that comes from being hit. This pain, which stuck with me stubbornly, wasn't the same as any other pain I had felt up to this point. Other pains slowly hurt less and less, but this one was gradually getting stronger, racking my whole body. I pressed firmly at the center of the pain, but this didn't have any effect. They stopped kicking me, and when I looked around I didn't see them. I tried to stand up but couldn't. I sensed a warm liquid touching my hand. I also felt this same liquid dripping from my forehead, spreading across my eyebrows and temples.

I stood up with great difficulty and tried to walk. Along with the shaking of my body, the fog around me was also shaking. I could only walk a few steps before I collapsed again. It was as if my stomach had been stabbed with something. The smell of a rotten wound was emanating from it. It felt as though the whole world were becoming hotter, as if it were on fire. And then suddenly the temperature dropped rapidly. My whole being began to tremble from the cold. This icy coldness started from my feet. It was very silent around me, but I could hear the voice that I only heard in the midst of chaos even in the midst of this silence. The distant voice gradually came closer to me.

All the blood from my body seemed to be stuck in the spot where I was wounded. It seemed like it was constricted by this blockage. The pain was spreading away from the blood stoppage, in the opposite direction, making me feel like my whole body was being wounded. As the pain entered my brain, I tried to alleviate it by clenching my teeth. But although I clenched my teeth as hard as I could, it had no effect. I had tasted pain many times before. But I never imagined that pain could take on a form this extreme. Due to the direction of its force, it seemed as though lying face down in the cold would help to alleviate the pain, and so I rocked onto that side, pressing it against the ground. It seemed completely impossible to alleviate the pain. I thought that if all of the blood in my body flowed out, the pain would become fainter, since the pain seemed to be related to the constriction of the blood in my veins. If that constriction went away, maybe the pain would disappear as well. Wanting to allow the blood to flow freely, I tried to loosen my hand from the place where it was flowing out with burning heat between my fingers. But I couldn't release my hand from that place; my hand seemed to be frozen.

I felt as though I might have to crawl somewhere else. Even though I didn't recognize anyone, I wanted to search for somebody. I started to crawl. I didn't know why I couldn't stand up. I had no choice but to crawl. It was all the same no matter which direction I moved. So I just crawled forward in a random direction. I don't know how far I went but after a while I just collapsed.

My eyes were becoming vague. With the gradually dimming vision in my eyes, I suddenly saw the number I was looking for. I focused my strength on the remaining vision in my eyes and looked at the number. The number was written so clearly. Surprised, I thought, *Why couldn't I find it before?* Had I not seen it even though I had passed in front of it? This was impossible. I had looked at every house and not missed a single number. The gate beside the number was firmly closed. Its iron bars were very thick and heavy duty, as though to block people's fantasies. This number was different from other numbers. It was carved into a golden piece of tin and could be seen very clearly by the eye. Under the number was written the words: "Psychiatric Hospital." I was shocked that this was the place I had been looking for so desperately.

My body seemed to be melding with the icy ground into a single substance. The scene in front of my eyes was becoming dimmer. I saw a few people's shoes coming toward me. As they moved slowly toward me, the memories in my mind also seemed to move toward me. I stretched my hands out toward them, but their shoes just walked past me, almost touching my face. Another person jumped over my head. Then my eyes became even vaguer, and I couldn't see anything. Just the sound of shoes and *that* sound, gradually coming closer until it could be heard very clearly. I recognized the sound as the sound of my mother's voice. She was calling my name in a long, drawn-out way.

Written in Ürümchi in 1990–1991.
Revised in Ürümchi in 2005.
Typed in Beijing and finished at 9 p.m. on February 15, 2006.
Revised version finalized in Ürümchi at 12:30 a.m. on March 7,
  2015